Ishmael is married to Irene and has three children, Joseph, Daniel and Suzy. He is an elder of Arun Community Church, on the Pioneer Team and a member of the Evangelical Alliance.

By the same author:

Children of the Voice 3

Descent into Nochurch

ISHMAEL

KINGSWAY PUBLICATIONS

EASTBOURNE

ISBN 0 85476 349 X

Produced by Bookprint Creative Services
P.O. Box 827, BN23 6NX, England for
KINGSWAY PUBLICATIONS LTD
Lottbridge Drove, Eastbourne, E Sussex BN23 6NT.
Printed in Great Britain

Contents

The story so far . . .

Children of the Voice introduces us to Little
Trouble—a rebellious kid in Oldchurch. He has lots
of questions that no one wants to answer: why do
Sundays have to be so boring? Why can't the kids
be at the same meeting as the grown-ups? Who is
the Voice? And why doesn't he speak to anyone so
they can hear him? Now that he is twelve years old
he decides to find some answers for himself.
Promising to return he sets off into the Bigwide-
world, where he meets Angela, Hearthunter,
Miraclekid and many other Children of the Voice.
He also meets the Enemy Superpowers, and one in
particular called Greedy Gutrot, who are out to try
and destroy him.

After many adventures he commits himself to
becoming a follower of the Voice, changes his
name to Little Christian, and with a small
team returns to Oldchurch . . . with devastating
consequences.

In *Children of the Voice 2*—The Invasion of
Newchurch—Little Christian is now nearly fifteen
and a leader in the very successful Newchurch.
Greedy Gutrot and the Enemy Superpowers decide
to invade Newchurch by enlisting some fake
followers of the Voice. These evil robots cause havoc
and chaos in Newchurch and completely fool all the
Children of the Voice . . . all except Little Christian,
that is.

Little Christian seeks to combat the invaders and

save Newchurch, but none of his friends agree, and as the battle reaches a climax it is no longer just a battle between the robots and the Children of the Voice—now it's Little Christian against the rest.

By the time Newchurch comes to its senses, Little Christian has been thrown out, and even Angela, his closest friend, thinks of him as a murderer.

Now read on!

I

The Runaway

It never rains but it pours, and now it really was pouring. The once-solid path had turned into a squelchy, gooey, brown, muddy stream and even the enormous giant oak trees that towered high, trying to protect Runaway Forest from such a deluge just stood looking sad, as their huge branches, like long sagging arms, allowed the torrential downpour to lash against the ground.

Though his trainers were saturated, his jeans soaked and his leather jacket unable to prevent ice-cold water from seeping down the back of his neck,

Little Christian rushed on. Nothing was going to make him slow down.

'I don't need them,' he mumbled to himself angrily for the hundredth time. 'Anyway, why should I forgive them after all the lousy things they said about me? It's all very well for Miraclekid, he's their hero. I mean, it wouldn't have been so bad if it was just Harmony and Rhoda Skateboard who had a crack at me. After all, they are just a couple of stupid girls, but my mates Hearthunter and Buddy, how could they even think such things about me, their leader? Well let's see how they cope with leading Newchurch without me.'

Then, as it always did, his mind went back to Angela and tears filled his eyes. 'Angela,' he continued bitterly, 'she proved to be the worst of the lot. Called me a murderer, said she never wanted to talk to me again. Well, her wishes have come true. I never want to set eyes on her again. She can go and marry Greedy Gutrot as far as I am concerned. They are two of a kind.'

'Oi!' a voice suddenly shouted.

Little Christian jumped out of his angry dreamworld and looking to his left he saw a rather well-dressed old man sheltering next to a fire under a huge rock.

'What do you want?' shouted Little Christian, rudely.

'Hey, no need to get stroppy,' said the old man. 'I just thought you might like to come under my shelter and dry off. I've got a nice hot cup of coffee over here which would warm you up a bit.'

Little Christian was not in any hurry to get anywhere. In fact he hadn't a clue where he was heading. All he wanted to do was to get as far away from Newchurch as he could. So he wandered over and sat down next to the old chap.

'Hello,' said the old chap, smiling. 'My name's Ron, Ron Guidance. What's yours?'

'Oh, I'm Little Chris . . . .' Then Little Christian paused. For the first time in his life he was suddenly embarrassed by his name. Then he continued, 'I'm Little Chris.'

'Well, nice to meet you, Little Chris,' said Ron, handing him a mug of coffee. As Ron stared at the fire saying nothing, Little Christian stared at Ron. He must have been in his sixties and wore a black hat partly covering short, grey hair and had a well-trimmed grey moustache. A long black coat went right down to his shoes which, although clean, had a layer of mud surrounding the soles and heels. He looked the opposite to Little Christian, which made Little Christian feel even more scruffy, dirty and angry.

Then Ron looked into Little Christian's face. 'What, may I ask, are you doing out in the middle of Runaway Forest on a day like this?'

'Mind your own business, you nosey old duffer,' shouted Little Christian, as his uncontrollable anger began to flare up again.

'Oh, I'm ever so sorry,' said old Ron politely. 'I didn't mean to pry. You're right, it's nothing to do with me.'

Little Christian was both surprised and ashamed that he should have reacted in such a way, and he apologised. He felt desperate to talk to someone and as there was no one else around except Ron, he guessed it might as well be him who felt the bitter edge of his fury. He explained that he was once one of the Children of the Voice and the leader of

Newchurch, but things had gone wrong and he had been falsely accused of all sorts of terrible things by people who were once his best friends. Now he just wanted to get as far away from them as possible.

Ron sat quietly—he didn't say a thing—and even the expression on his face didn't give away what he was feeling. Little Christian remembered his early days in Oldchurch, how he was taught that it was sensible to listen to the wisdom of older and wiser people. Although he didn't know if Ron was wiser, he was sure that he was older, so he asked Ron if he had any advice to give.

Ron Guidance stared at him. After a few moments he slowly started to speak, quietly at first, but getting louder by the sentence. 'Beware of impersonators. They may look good, they may sound good, but they are no good. The ones you have left behind are not genuine. You are right to be leaving them. You don't need them. In fact you don't need anybody except the Voice. Look at me, alone as a fish in a fruitshop—but happy, yes, there is no one happier than me.

'I too follow the Voice, only not in such a fanatical way as your ex-friends do, and it's not by chance that the Voice has put me here in your path to give you advice and direction.' Now in full swing, Ron stood up and started waving his arms around like he was conducting an orchestra of millions.

'You have no choice, Little Chris. You can't go back. You must go on. Every man is an island. Don't allow yourself to become close friends with anyone else, or you will only end up getting hurt again. Listen closely to the advice of Ron Guidance. It's as reliable as the Manual itself.' After a pause he brought his face very close to Little Christian's.

'Furthermore,' he continued in a breathy whisper, 'I suggest you make your way to a city called Nochurch—a wonderful place where many Voice followers who are fed up with being accountable go and find the freedom they need. Once you are there, ask for directions to Sativision House and ask for a close friend of mine called Hugo Yourway.

He paused. 'You know, I believe the Voice wants to make you a star.'

Ron then drew away from Little Christian and sat down again mumbling, 'Here endeth the first lesson.'

This was just the advice Little Christian wanted to hear. After thanking Ron he left the shelter of the rock and the warmth of the fire and returned to the cold rain, still bucketing down, but now he didn't feel quite so angry. Now he felt like he was on a sort of commission for the Voice.

2

The Secret Sixty-Five

'I would like to call this meeting to order,' came a polite voice from a very tall, very thin man with a black moustache which underlined his large, widely-spread nose. 'It gives me great pleasure to welcome you all to this meeting of the Grand Order Of Secretly Evil Yobs, affectionately known to us all as "GOOSEY".' His listeners smiled nervously in response. The thin man's stomach made a noisy rumbling sound as he glanced around the large, cold, sparsely-furnished Oddboys' Hall, with its old stained-glass windows and its sixty-five (including himself) all male Goosey members present.

It is worth noting that when Goosey members met together on occasions such as these they were known as a 'gaggle', and they took themselves very seriously. They would be very offended if they heard anyone giggle about the gaggle of gooseys gathering.

Of course being a secret society no non-Goosey would be allowed to gatecrash a gaggle gathering as two huge, musclebound Goosey guards, known as 'Pecks', stood to attention by both the main door and the fire exit. Now if an outsider had managed to peep around the door, they may have found it hard to take any of the Gooseys seriously. You see, the Gooseys all sat around long scruffy tressel tables looking immaculate in their black dinner jackets, white silk shirts and red bow ties, but if you peeped under the tables you would see that instead of wearing trousers they wore bright yellow shorts, with grey thermal socks and black flippers over their feet. This, believe it or not, was what distinguished the Gooseys from all other mere mortals.

'It seems like an eternity has passed since we last met,' continued the mouth below the moustache, 'and I, being your Grand Gander, bring you tidings of great joy. As you know, the perfect gaggle number for a very large city is 666. However, for a city of our size, the number should be sixty-six and for a long time we have had to function minus one goosey.' The gaggle all stared at their leader, hoping their faces were portraying an expression that he would find pleasing.

'Permission to speak!' shouted Rip Emoff, who was the owner of the Nochurch Casino.

'Yes, Rip,' said Grand Gander.

'Well, regarding our late beloved member, rumour

has it that one of us around this table ran off with Amos Onmyturf's Lesserbreed, which caused Amos to go raving mad, which drove him to dumping his Littlekid in the middle of Runaway Forest and sadly to top himself.'

'Rip, please sit down and be quiet!' ordered Grand Gander, feeling embarrassed, as he tried again to forget the slight indiscretion involving himself and Amos' attractive wife. 'We have discussed this many times before and I am convinced that none of you would do such a terrible thing to a fellow Goosey as to steal his own personal Lesserbreed. And remember, it was I who heroically saved his female Littlekid and persuaded her to work for us—and where would you all be without her? (Ahem.) Now, to business!

The Gooseys all smiled and agreed that Grand Gander was right. Amos Onmyturf's female Littlekid kept their slave-trade thriving.

'If I may continue,' continued Grand Gander. 'Alas, Amos is no more, so we need our sixty-sixth member. Well, the good news is a short while ago a new citizen moved into our community, and since then he has gained the respect of many, including myself.'

The gaggle looked nervously at each other, unsure of how to respond, as they had become very secure with just the sixty-five.

'Permission to speak?' asked Bigsby Bankbalance, a local bank manager of the Stashitaway Bank.

'Of course, Bigsby,' replied Grand Gander.

'Money is my life,' boasted Bigsby, 'and I judge a man's credentials by his credits—cashwise, if you know what I mean. Is this person of sound financial standing, because we don't want any poor people in our company? In my professional opinion they are more trouble than they are worth, hence my expression . . .' at which point all the gaggle joined in, having heard it so many times before, 'If not rich . . . ditch.'

'I assure you the person I have in mind is very wealthy, Bigsby, and unlike some he has not found the need to print his own notes.' Bigsby blushed. 'However, I'm sure he could be persuaded to use your bank if he became one of us,' added Grand Gander with a twinkle in his eye that Bigsby liked.

'Permission to speak?' asked Major Snob-Value.

'Yes, Major,' said Grand Gander.

'I say, Gander old chap, is this person of reputable employment and can he be trusted to be totally silent regarding our affairs?' He paused. 'I can't abide those working and lower classes; they have no breeding, and there is more chance of water-skiing behind the Titanic than there is of one of them keeping their mouths shut.'

Before Grand Gander could answer, or the gaggle nod in agreement, Chauvinist Pigg, a member who was born overseas somewhere but who would never reveal his nationality, interrupted by saying that he hoped they were not discussing allowing one of the Lesserbreed (the Gooseys' affectionate term for the female gender) to enlist. As Chauvinist continued, not only would they be unable to cope intellectually, but they really would have nothing to contribute once taken out of their kitchens.

The Gaggle all nodded in agreement.

Grand Gander attempted a smile, which was his first attempt for a month. 'I think we all agree with your sentiments, Major. This person has a very secure employment and has got to where he is today thanks to his utmost discretion.' Then he looked at Chauvinist condescendingly. 'You are not in some remote jungle now, my friend. You are part of our great country. You must be very careful what you say about the Lesserbreed, or people will start thinking that we Gooseys are sexist. Most of you chose to marry one, and not only do they carry out their domestic chores admirably, they also spend time with your Littlekids allowing you to forget that you've even got any. No, we are not here to put down the Lesserbreed, but we are here to say that their place is in the living quarters and not here with us.'

'Hear, hear!' shouted the Major. 'Er, that is, I mean *not* here, here,' he stammered, correcting himself.

'Permission to speak?' asked Al Kidsarbrats, a head-teacher from the exclusive Boffinswot School.

'Yes,' came the reply from the leader's chair.

'You mentioned Littlekids. I hate them. Your new member: he's not too young, is he? After all, I have these horrible Littlekid louts ruining every day of my life. I couldn't bear the thought of having to sit facing one as a member of our beloved gaggle.'

The gaggle all nodded again.

Grand Gander tried a second smile, but again failed miserably, just as his stomach made an even louder gurgling sound. 'Well actually,' he said loudly, trying to overpower what sounded like a war going on inside him, 'he is young—in fact very young—but before you all panic and think that your esteemed leader is turning our beloved gaggle into some Littlekids' playpark, take my word for it, this Littlekid is not only very mature, but in some areas is more experienced than I am.'

All the gaggle gasped at the prospect that it was

possible for anyone to have more experience in anything than Grand Gander.

'Any more questions?' asked Grand Gander, hoping there weren't, as he was growing very impatient and was hating democracy more and more by the minute. He was dying to tell the gaggle the name of the one they all kept asking questions about, but he also knew it was right they had their say before he did so.

'Just a quick one,' came the almost hiss-like whisper of Arthur Theist. 'What is it, A?' enquired Grand Gander, knowing that Arthur hated the name Arthur and preferred to be called by his initial A.

'Well,' squeaked A, 'this person hasn't got any strong, dangerous beliefs, has he? We all know our beloved constitution requires us to be good religious citizens who are not allowed to believe in anything, except the Gooseys of course. This new member hasn't been contaminated by any Voice followers, has he?'

The gaggle gasped an even greater gasp than last time.

'I think I know our constitution, A,' muttered Grand Gander, now not even attempting a smile. 'After all, I did write it, didn't I?' he said angrily. 'Furthermore, seeing that you made mention of my beloved rules, may I also remind you that you have just broken one. Rule one, subsection A, clearly states that the word you have just offended us with must never be used at a Goosey meeting. Any reference to the aforementioned person must be simply V.'

The Grand Gander stood tall and put a black hat on. 'A Theist,' he bellowed, 'all rule-breakers must be punished. Pecks, do your thing.'

As one Peck grabbed hold of the hissing A and bent him over the tressle table, the other took off a flipper. 'How many, Grand Gander?' shouted the Peck.

'Oh, six of the flipper should be adequate,' snarled Grand Gander, who had now calmed down a bit.

As heavy rubber whacked the even heavier rump, A Theist wailed loudly. The gaggle enjoyed the entertainment and Grand Gander pondered the good old days when the answer to any mischief was always a good whack on the backside.

Six slaps and six screams later the Pecks were back guarding their doors, the Grand Gander was ready to continue and A Theist was back hovering over his seat as it was a bit painful to sit on it.

'Now,' said Grand Gander, 'back to where we were before we were so rudely interrupted.' Then, to everyone's utter surprise, he burst out laughing. Without more ado he spluttered, 'The person I am proposing to you was . . . wait for it, A . . . once the leader of the opposition, yes Newchurch.'

The gaggle gave vent to the loudest gasp of the day. Some even fell off their chairs and hid under the tables as they feared the name Newchurch nearly as much as the name Voice. The Pecks, whose highlight of the meeting had been to punish A, were still reliving those moments and not paying attention. They wondered what was happening and rushed around the hall thinking they were being invaded.

'However,' continued Grand Gander, still managing such a wide grin that his moustache looked horizontal, 'you will be pleased to hear that he has now seen the dark . . . and had his eyes well and truly closed.'

'Prove it,' whimpered all the shivering gaggle together.

The tall, thin leader put his hand inside his jacket pocket and pulled out a small business card. 'Read this!' he snapped, and just as he was about to hand it to Rob Emall, a high-class thief who sat on his right, to pass round, his stomach let out such an earth-shattering roar that anything made of glass, ranging from the beautiful stained-glass windows to Major Snob-Value's monocle, smashed into millions of tiny pieces with the vibration. The now totally confused Pecks rushed up to Grand Gander telling him to get under the table and they would soon find out who had detonated the bomb that they had just heard exploding.

All was raging chaos, so Grand Gander grabbed hold of each tressle table and, screaming, 'Shhuutt uupp!' at the top of his voice, threw them, one at a time, the whole length of the hall, breaking anything or anyone that got in their way.

Eventually everyone calmed down, and with no tables left to hide under they quietly sat back on their seats and even the Pecks returned to their doors.

'I do beg your pardon,' said Grand Gander composing himself. 'There's no bomb, Pecks. I've recently changed my eating habits and my stomach seems to be objecting. You could say it's making its feelings audibly known.

'Now, read this, Rob, then pass it on.'

As they read it they started to smile; very, very confident smiles.

'Now we've no worries here,' they laughed.

'Even old A Theist has more faith than this character,' shouted one.

'Yeah, the most influential loser I've ever heard of,' shrieked another.

'So I take it you agree that my choice has all the necessary qualifications to become one of us?' asked Grand Gander.

'He's almost over-qualified,' shouted a voice hysterically and all went into fits of totally uncontrollable laughter. Even the Pecks started to laugh, although of course they had no idea what they were laughing about.

Again the noise eventually subsided, and being a true democracy a vote was taken and all agreed that the proposed person should be approached and invited to be initiated at the next meeting, which would be at the earliest possible convenience, allowing time for the necessary repairs to be done to the Oddboys' Hall and new tables and windows to be purchased.

'Now for the final few items on our agenda,' said Grand Gander looking at a sheet of paper that had nothing written on it. 'Pat, over to you.'

Pat Rolman, the crooked police officer, opened up a sheet of paper and started reading his report, which mentioned all the progress being made on the Gooseys' illegal money-making ventures. 'Drug-trafficking trade doing very well; extortion rackets are growing daily. Let's see . . .' he continued. 'Oh yes, the membership of the Muckybooks and Violent Videos lending library has multiplied at an enormous rate, especially now we have encouraged Littlekids to join.' And so his list continued. 'One other important piece of news is that Chief Officer Kleencop and the city police still have no idea that we Gooseys are responsible for all Nochurch's major unsolved crimes.' All the Gooseys laughed together at the thought of the weak and useless boys in blue.

'Thank you, Pat. I would like to mention our Littlekid slave-trade,' said Grand Gander, again taking the floor as this was a responsibility he had chosen to oversee himself.

All the gaggle listened very intently. This was of great interest to them because by exporting slaves they had all become very rich, and by holding onto a few for their own convenience it had made them all men of leisure. 'Our ally in Runaway Forest is doing a grand job in providing us with these troublesome, discontented Littlekids, and the next person to visit her will tell her so on my behalf.'

'Excuse me, Grand Gander, permission to speak.'

'Yes, Bigsby, what is it?'

'Well, whose turn is it to collect the next slave, er, I mean Littlekid?'

Grand Gander thought. 'I believe that it's the Major next, then you after him. You can collect the horse and cart from Boffinswot School, because as we all remember from our last meeting Al offered to house both of them for us.'

All seemed satisfied.

After a few very minor items were discussed, like who was giving whom a lift home, the meeting closed in the usual way, with all the gaggle holding hands and singing 'Goosey Goosey Gander' and the Pecks frogmarching everybody out of the building.

Grand Gander sat back contentedly in the deserted, almost-decimated Oddboys' Hall. It felt good having all the most influential people from Nochurch under his control, but all sixty-four around the table meant nothing to him compared to the one name written upon this business card. As he continued to stare at it he couldn't resist reading it out loud.

Little Chris (TV star)
1 Hopelesscase Mansion
Nochurch
Code: WHO AMI

Then Grand Gander looked at the small words at the bottom which looked almost insignificant, yet to him were the most important.

Minister of Nochurch

Again the thin man managed a smile. 'Little Chris—or should I say Little Christian—you can call me Grand Gander when you first meet me. I doubt if you will live long enough to call me GG.' He chuckled, then he laughed until he ached, all the time waving the little card in his hand. 'But you'll never be around long enough to know who I really am.'

Tears rolled down his face. 'I'm really looking forward to meeting you,' he choked. 'My dad has told me a lot about you. I wonder if you will notice any family resemblance, like he's so fat and I'm so thin.'

Suddenly his face became serious. 'Where my fat father failed, I won't! Little Christian' I am going to destroy you . . . for ever.'

As Grand Gander got up to leave, a thin Oldie wearing a long coat and a hat crept into the hall, staying in the shadows.

'Oh, there you are,' said Grand Gander. 'How come you have taken so long to get here? I wondered when you were going to show up.'

Not getting a reply, he pulled out a large brown

envelope that was full of bank notes. 'Here,' he shouted, 'take this. You're doing a wonderful job.'

As the thin man caught the flying envelope and started to creep back out of the hall, Grand Gander shouted after him, 'Meet me outside here after the next Goosey meeting. I'll let you know when it is. I've got a very important assignment for you.'

The man nodded and left. Grand Gander wandered into the middle of the deserted hall and started to do a little dance by himself. 'Life is so easy,' he thought. 'Life is so good. I am so proud of myself.'

The unearthly inhuman noise that followed as Grand Gander danced around the hall is beyond description. Suffice it to say that his stomach was crying out to be filled. It was time to go and give it a treat.

3

Headaches and Heartache

It had been a long, long night and by the way things were going it seemed like the night would never end.

'Aw, come on now, Buddy, there's no time like the present. It's time to go for it,' shouted Hearthunter with all the enthusiasm of a power-packed preacher prophesying over a park full of pagan people.

'Yeah, it's like time to see the blind man leap clean out of his wheelchair,' added Miraclekid getting his metaphors slightly mixed up in his excitement.

'Well, I don't really know,' replied Buddy the

Flockwatcher cautiously, while scratching his head with one hand and twiddling a pen that had the words 'The Hesitator Gets There Later' inscribed on it in the other. 'Let me just read to you once more the points that I spent a lot of time meditating on last week.'

Just as Miraclekid was about to shout, 'Not again!' Hearthunter slapped a hand over his mouth and only a gurgling sound came out.

'Point number one: the Voice has been really good to us undeserving Littlekids of Newchurch, and thanks to him we have grown incredibly numerically, especially over the past year.' At this stage he walked over to his office wall where an enormous graph, which was so long it looked like a frieze on the wallpaper, displayed these facts. The graph was covered with all sorts of different coloured pen lines seemingly going in all directions. Apart from looking pretty these lines meant absolutely nothing to Hearthunter and Miraclekid, but to Buddy they held as much fascination as the Orient Express would to a Tibetan train-spotter.

'Point number two: to plant a Newchurch in Religios-city is of course part of our long-term strategy, but are we being a little premature? And finally, point number three (all good Flockwatchers have three points): our long long-term project, which is to try and restore some of the lost loners of Nochurch, well I have to say that I don't think any of us are ready for that yet.' Then, with a solemn voice he continued, 'It was not so long ago that our own future was in the balance.'

'You speak for yourself!' yelled Miraclekid. 'I never questioned my future.' His voice always grew louder when he was arguing about something that he felt passionately about. 'If we don't move out till we are ready, we shall still be here having this conversation when the Voice returns. You're sounding more like a staid boring Oldchurch pastor than a life-packed, vision-smacked child of the Voice. I've had enough of talking about strategy and projects. I say it's time to do the business.'

To Miraclekid's annoyance, Buddy always refused to get worked up—it was not in his nature—so his voice continued with the same monotone that it always had.

'I may seem staid to you, but I and many of my flock would call it stability. I may also seem boring,' he continued, 'to one as impetuous as your good self, but I believe before we "do the business" we should spend much time in planning, prayer, familiarising and fasting which are words that never seem to be in your vocabulary.'

'In other words we must do things in the Voice's timing and not ours.'

Miraclekid and Hearthunter just sat quietly. Neither attempted to argue with Buddy's theology or logic, because due to the many hours he spent in preparation, prayer and study at his desk he did seem to know more about the deeper truths in the Manual than they did.

Buddy also went quiet because deep down he wished that he had the excitement and zeal of Miraclekid and Hearthunter, and the last thing he wanted to do was to quell their enthusiasm. They all stared at each other. Eventually Buddy stared back at his graph and Miraclekid stared at his watch, so Hearthunter broke the silence.

'I think maybe we are all right and the Voice deliberately made us to think and act differently so that together we sort of balance each other out, whereas separated we would either never get round to doing anything or else we would just be racing around and doing a lot, but probably not really achieving anything.'

Buddy and Miraclekid nodded in agreement, both pleased to end the disagreement and both fed up with staring at graphs and watches. 'All right,' said Buddy, 'it looks like we need a bit of a compromise if we leaders are to move on together. How would you feel if we were to keep praying about the Nochurch loners at present and in the meantime make a hit into Religios-city?'

Miraclekid and Hearthunter leapt up and down with excitement.

'Also,' continued Buddy, 'while you are recruiting your hit squad to take with you, I will pay a visit to the leaders of any Oldchurches that may be already there. It's so important we don't just rush in, but let them know about our mission, as there may be things we can do together.'

Hearthunter again spoke up: 'Having done my homework already on Religios-city, I'm afraid any sort of co-operation seems very unlikely. I have discovered that there are two Oldchurches in existence. One is called the Ancient Church of the Thirteenth Male Apostle and the other is called the Modern Movement of the Free Sisters' Fellowship, and both hate each other so much they have declared an all-out war with each other.'

'Oh dear,' exclaimed Buddy. 'Not so good. Still, we must do things properly, so I'll arrange a meeting with them first thing tomorrow morning.'

Miraclekid and Hearthunter were now very excited and Buddy was as near excitement as his personality would allow him to be. They decided to spend what was left of the now short, short night praising the Voice together. Leadership was important, but leaders being real friends seemed even more important. They felt very secure knowing that their love and respect for each other went far deeper than any disagreement that they might ever have.

While all these exciting things were happening in the Newchurch office another Littlekid was restlessly trying to sleep in one of the small Newchurch houses. This Littlekid had not had a good peaceful night's sleep for a long time. Neither had she allowed a smile or any outward show of happiness to be seen on her pretty young face for the same period. She was still part of Newchurch in as much as she lived there and attended various events that took place, but her heart was far from being the exuberant Voice director that she was once known as. Everyone who looked at her could see that she was different. No longer did she talk to the Voice or listen to him or even read the Manual. She was even rumoured to have said that sometimes she doubted if the Voice existed.

As this overtired young female Littlekid tossed and turned restlessly in her bed, she accidently bumped against her bedside cupboard and a framed photograph fell onto the carpeted floor with a gentle thud. Immediately she sat bolt upright in her bed. It had had the same effect as an alarm bell screaming in her ears. She leaned over, and by the help of the moonlit night slowly picked it up off the floor. She sat there motionless, holding it next to her heart as she had done each evening for as long as she cared to remember. She clutched it tightly, as if her life depended on it, but she didn't weep. The fact was that her eyes had cried so much and for so long, there seemed to be no tears left for her to shed. The once emotional Littlekid now seemed unable to let any emotions show.

After a while, the birds outside her window heralded the soft light of a brand new day and she slowly took the photograph away from her body and directed her eyes at it. There they were, two very happy young Littlekids who seemed to have not a care in the world. They looked as though they were very close friends and maybe even loved each other.

As the dawn sun stretched up and its warm light crept through her window she glanced at her dressing-table mirror on the far side of her bedroom. Looking back at the photo she could hardly believe that the Littlekid in the photo was the same person she was staring at in the mirror.

The stress and strain of months of heartbreak and broken fellowship with the Voice had taken their toll and made the Littlekid look older and more haggard than any normal Voice follower of her age. Her face was drawn and pale and her body thin. She had no interest in food.

Guilt had become her master and she had become its slave. It had taken control of her life. As she gazed at the photo and the young male Littlekid standing beside her, she again pondered the fact that it was she who had falsely accused him of all sorts of terrible things. She wondered where he was now. She had heard nothing from him since that terrible day when he had walked out of Newchurch. She didn't know if he was dead or alive, but then she didn't really know if she was.

Over the next few days Hearthunter and Miraclekid were totally hyperactive and rushing around everywhere sharing the exciting news of the hit squad invading Religios-city with all of Newchurch so they too would catch the excitement and start praying for it. They decided to take three of the young Littlekids with them: Ivor Future, Joy Atalltimes and Hope Itgoeswell. Buddy agreed with their choice as he too felt that these three had great potential and it would be a chance for Hearthunter and Miraclekid to train them up while on the battlefield, so to speak.

Buddy told Hearthunter and Miraclekid that he had arranged to meet both Canon Blast from the Ancient Church of the Thirteenth Male Apostle and Pastor Kitchen from the Modern Movement of the Free Sisters' Fellowship the following day, then if all went well their hit squad could burst into action the following Monday. He felt it right that all Newchurch should pray over them on the previous Sunday.

As all seemed to be decided, Hearthunter started to say, 'What a shame . . .' but before he could finish his sentence he was interrupted by Buddy, 'Don't say any more,' he whispered with tears welling up in his eyes. 'I know what you are about to say. She has been loved, prayed for and given advice, but she has chosen to lock herself away so that no one, not even the Voice, has been able to get to her. I sometimes wonder if she will ever allow herself to be put right or be used by the Voice again.'

Miraclekid stayed silent for once and just looked down at his trainers. He too had unsuccessfully prayed for her, but he knew enough about miracles to know that unless she opened herself up and allowed the Voice to heal her, nothing could stop the self-destruction of this his old best friend's girlfriend. What would become of Angela?

4

Big on the Box

As the illuminated sign of Nochurch Police Station swung gently in the breeze, Chief Kleencop paced his office floor punching his right fist into the palm of his left hand in frustration. 'The crime rate of this city is rocketing, yet I can't do anything about it,' he grumbled to himself. 'I know all those bigwigs who call themselves Gooseys are behind it all, but they are the cleverest, most influential people around. How am I, a simple cop, ever going to find enough evidence to nail them?'

'Fancy a coffee, Chief?' came a voice through the

door. 'Yes thanks, Pat,' said the chief. 'It's good to know I've got at least one cop with me who is one hundred per cent trustworthy.'

Pat smiled to himself as he walked towards the coffee machine.

The heat was blistering as the bright spotlights shone in the small studio. 'Take one!' shouted a rather effeminate voice from behind a large double-glazed soundproofed window that looked like it should have had fish swimming around in it. At this cue a tall young man on the far side of the window stood up from a black swivel chair and walked over to a large black microphone. The youth was immaculately dressed in a shiny bright blue suit, with a shiny pink silk shirt which had a shiny red tie hanging from beneath the collar. Red nylon socks were just noticeable between the trouser turnups and the shiny white leather shoes. His hair was immaculate, gelled down so not one strand could wander out of place, and the make-up covering the face was just enough to give a tanned rather than scorched appearance.

The mouth opened just a few inches away from the microphone to display a set of teeth that were so white and shiny that one could have thought that they had just been covered with a thick coat of high gloss white paint. Then up from the throat, over the tongue and booming out between the teeth these words broke loose: 'Now listen carefully, viewers, or should I say, my friends. I'm not just asking you. No, I'm not even just telling you. I am in fact ordering you not to stop watching me if you really want to hear what the Voice wants to say to you this very night.'

Camera 2 moved in nearer to do a close-up of his face, which due to the intense heat of the lights had started to perspire and was becoming as shiny as the clothes he was wearing. 'Yea, verily within the next hour,' the voice continued, 'I am going to explain to you not only why you need to know the Voice as your best friend, but also for a very small donation towards my ministry, how you, whoever you are or whatever you have done wrong, can also become his friend and become almost as Voice-like as myself.'

With the foundations laid, the preach then continued non-stop (except for various commercial breaks to advertise the speaker's specially-anointed videotapes and cassettes from previous programmes) for fifty-five minutes.

The face behind a million viewers' television screens would sometimes laugh, sometimes weep, but always yell into the microphone.

While the cameramen were racing around the studio like there was no tomorrow, shooting from every conceivable angle to try and keep the viewers' attention, the lighting changed after every twenty swallows from the speaker's adam's apple a bit like a sound-to-light disco.

Then came those last crucial five minutes. Success or failure would be determined in those all-important 300 seconds. 'And now,' the mouth concluded so dramatically that in comparison the world's number one ranking Shakespearian actor would have sounded like an amateur, 'I've not just shared my heart with you. Nay, I have given you my all.' At this cue a technician from the other side of the double-glazing pressed a button that released the sounds of organ music followed by what could only be described as voices sounding like they'd just passed an audition to become part of an angelic choir.

'And why?' agonised the voice. 'And why?' it repeated a little louder. 'Because . . . I love you.' Tears came rolling down the makeup-covered cheeks as they did every week at this point of the programme, and his head bowed. For the first time in an hour he whispered, which caught the sound crew off guard and sent the million viewers rushing for their remote controls to turn the volume level up. 'Good-bye. May the Voice bless you, and have a nice day.'

As tears stopped rolling in the television studio, tears continued rolling in the homes of two million bloodshot eyes. No one dared switch off their sets. It was as though they had all become hypnotised by a small electrical plastic box which communicated with them, but would not permit them to communicate with it.

The credits rolled in front of them in wonderful flowery Olde English italics, then afterwards came these words: 'Little Chris has told you everything, but it is vital that you remember what he has taught you. Send $40 immediately to the following address and receive your very own personal videotape of this programme. Remember, the first 10,000 cheques to arrive will all receive their very own handkerchiefs that Little Chris has personally wept in. So don't delay, write in today.' Then followed Little Chris's address and finally, like the Amen, the words: 'All major credit cards accepted.'

The studio crew relaxed, another programme in the can. 'Well done, lovey,' congratulated Hugo Yourway, the rather camp programme producer, as he burst in through the studio door and approached

Little Chris, 'Oh my,' he continued, 'even I had a tear in my eye at one point. You really were very convincing today.'

'Wait a minute,' said Little Chris defensively picking up a towel and trying to scrape some of the make-up off his face. 'I really do believe in everything I say.'

'Oh, I am sure you do,' replied Hugo. 'You are one of the sweetest little Children of the Voice I have ever met. You have such a nice face even I nearly believed what you were saying.' With this Hugo went into one of his giggling fits which Little Chris found most embarrassing. He decided it was time to leave.

As he reached the door Hugo contained himself long enough to shout out, 'Good-bye, Chrissy. See you soon,' and then continued his high-pitched giggling.

Little Chris span round, his make-upless face red with anger. 'I am not Chrissy! I'm Little Chris!' he yelled furiously. 'And you'd better not forget it!' With that he slammed the studio door.

Hugo immediately stopped laughing, so offended he nearly burst into tears. 'Miserable, ungrateful little hypocrite,' he whispered under his breath. 'He seems to forget he was nothing until I discovered him. Ron Guidance sent me a wreck and I made him a star. It was I who taught him good dress sense and how to speak and perform in front of the camera. I made him all he is today. He may be able to fool two million viewers with his corny rhetoric, but if they knew him like I do, they would soon see that there is more chance of me being one of the Children of the Voice than him.'

As Little Chris left Sativision House he found a

crowd of female Littlekids waiting outside for him. Most wanted autographs, some wanted handkerchiefs and a few wanted a date with him that night. He was in no mood to be pleasant and just pushed them all roughly to one side and climbed into his large white chauffeur-driven limo. 'Home, driver,' he yelled rudely. Then he settled down to watch a video of his performance that afternoon.

It was exactly an hour later that his car pulled past the security guards standing next to the huge garden gates that led into his estate. He gazed at the beautiful ornate cross-shaped sign saying, 'One Hopeless Mansion' as the electronic gates glided open. The limo drove up the long driveway and the small round pebbles made a loud crunching noise as the huge wide tyres of the heavy vehicle tried to squash them flat. The sun was sinking fast behind the huge oak trees that were scattered all over the vast finely-cut lawn. Little Chris's garden may have looked unplanned to the experienced horticulturist. Nothing except the turf had been manhandled. All the rest of the garden was just like it was when he purchased it, wild and like a wilderness (which were two words Little Chris could relate to).

The large car stopped in front of the mansion, which stood like a great white castle with its ten en-suite bedrooms, three bathrooms, two lounges, a drawing room, library, offices, kitchen, plus of course the gym, swimming pool, jacuzzi and sauna. The modest sort of house every TV star who puts himself out for the Voice should have, thought Little Chris.

He stepped out of the car and, ignoring the chauffeur, climbed the twenty steps, walked between the two large mock Grecian pillars and eventually reached the large double wooden front doors. Fumbling in his pockets he eventually found his key, opened one of the huge doors and walked in, carefully shutting it behind him.

It was great to be home.

Before he was famous one of the most exciting times in the day was when the postman brought his post. Even if one morning the delivery was very early, the minute he heard the rattle of the letterbox and the gentle thud of envelopes hitting carpet, he was out of bed and downstairs like a rocket. But now it was slightly different. Once inside his hallway the first view that confronted him was three very large mail bags crammed with letters. Of course he had his own private office staff to open them, read them and answer them, but he still insisted on seeing the amount of incoming mail each day before anyone else touched it. His staff considered the reason was because he wanted to keep some sort of grassroots contact with the viewers, but Little Chris really did it to see if he was gaining or losing popularity.

Popularity brought prosperity and prosperity was what a person in his position needed to flaunt around to show everyone that he was in close touch with the Voice. Material wealth was a sign of spiritual achievement. Ninety-nine per cent of the envelopes would contain money from people who wanted to purchase his preaching products. If the number dropped dramatically, he would be in a very embarrassing position financially. All he had was rented, hired or on loan, though of course none of his admirers knew this.

Without the sackfuls of money, he would either be broke or have to do what he did a long time ago—trust the Voice to provide for him. Still, he mused, smiling to himself, three sackfuls was fine and about average. It would certainly pay off all the bills until next week.

Little Chris slipped out of his uncomfortable shoes and, walking over the luxurious deep spongelike carpet, poured himself a glass of Sacro Vino from his drinks cabinet. Nochurch really was a wonderful place to live, he thought to himself. It was the sort of place where a Voice follower could get on and do his thing for the Voice and not have to be answerable to anyone. It was great that Nochurch lived up to its name and had no churches. Who needed churches and interfering church leaders when you had the Voice? mused Little Chris in a vain attempt at theology.

It was then, as he turned around to go and sit in his favourite armchair, he noticed a very official envelope sitting on the mantelpiece above the blazing log fire. He assumed that this must have come by special delivery and that one of his staff must have put it there for his special attention. As he picked up the envelope he suddenly felt excited and his heart started beating faster. He couldn't understand why he should feel this way just by picking up a bit of paper. He hadn't felt this sort of feeling for a long time.

He sat down in his large black armchair and as he released a lever a footrest appeared. Carefully he put his drink down on the table next to him, then opened the envelope and began to read the letter.

As he gazed at it his eyes nearly popped out of his head in amazement and his heart beat so fast that it sounded like a runaway train. 'Wow!' he shouted as he leapt out of his chair and sent both table and drink flying. 'It's a miracle . . . thank you, Voice. Now at last I know I really have made the big time.'

5

The War of the Words

Buddy knew immediately that he had entered Religios-city. It was cold and uncaring and really miserable. He had walked past a big sign on the outskirts which read: 'YOU ARE NOT ALLOWED IN RELIGIOS-CITY UNLESS YOU OBEY OUR RULES.' 'They certainly have an interesting way of making people feel welcome,' he thought.

As he walked into the shopping centre he had never seen so many noticeboards and they all started with the words, 'YOU MUST NOT . . .' There was 'YOU MUST NOT LAUGH OR TELL JOKES ON

THE PAVEMENT.' Then there was 'YOU MUST NOT SMILE, GRIN, SMIRK OR SHOW ANY FORM OF HAPPINESS WHILE CROSSING THE ROAD.' Outside the shops were many more signs.

The butcher's shop said: 'YOU MUST NOT BRING VEGETARIANS INTO THIS SHOP.'

The greengrocer's said: 'YOU MUST NOT BRING CARNIVORES INTO THIS SHOP.'

The health food shop said: 'YOU MUST NOT BRING FAT PEOPLE INTO THIS SHOP.'

The fish and chip shop said: 'YOU MUST NOT BRING THIN PEOPLE INTO THIS SHOP.'

The fur coat shop said: 'YOU MUST NOT BRING ANIMALS INTO THIS SHOP.'

The pet shop said: 'YOU MUST NOT BRING HUMANS INTO THIS SHOP.'

The clothes shop said: 'YOU MUST NOT BRING YOUR NAKED BODY INTO THE SHOP.'

The cassette shop said: 'YOU MUST NOT PLAY MUSIC IN THE SHOP.'

The supermarket said: 'YOU MUST NOT BRING TROLLIES INTO THE SHOP.'

The toyshop said: 'YOU MUST NOT BRING CHILDREN INTO THE SHOP.'

The computer shop said: 'YOU MUST NOT BRING VIRUSES INTO THE SHOP.'

The shoe shop said: 'YOU MUST NOT BRING SMELLY FEET INTO THE SHOP.'

The bookshop said: 'YOU MUST NOT BRING WORMS INTO THE SHOP.'

And that was just to name a few.

Buddy was intrigued, and as he looked more closely he realised that each sign had the words: 'BY ORDER OF BLAST AND KITCHEN.'

'Wow!' thought Buddy. 'These Oldchurch leaders really do have a major influence in this town.'

But as strange as all these posters were, the strangest thing was that he had not seen a single person walking around. He had seen a few grumpy shopkeepers' faces staring at him from out of their windows, but apart from that it was as if he had entered a ghost town.

Seeing the chemist shop with the words, 'YOU MUST NOT TRUST HERBAL MEDICINES' written outside he went towards the door deciding to ask a lady he saw through the window to tell him how he could find Canon Blast's house. As he reached the door she ran up to it, bolted it and put a sign up saying: 'YOU MUST NOT ENTER—I'M CLOSED'. He tried a few more shops and exactly the same thing happened. Buddy was shocked. He was one of the most loving and friendly people you could wish to meet and he had never been treated like this before.

It was then he heard some loud chimes from a church bell, so he ran towards the sound as fast as he could. As the last clang of the old bell rang he found himself standing looking at the great old building that it was coming from. It was typical of an Oldchurch building, beautifully built hundreds of years ago with a wonderful historic attraction about it, but it would be hard to describe it as warm, cosy and friendly, which was the environment that Buddy was used to when meeting with the Newchurch people to worship the Voice.

'Oi! What the blazes do you want?' came a ferocious voice standing outside the main wooden doors of the old building, from a man dressed in a long black robe. Buddy nearly jumped out of his skin. It was the last thing he had expected to hear as he was day-dreaming and gazing at the magnificent old building. 'Oh,' he said, 'I'm looking for the Ancient Church of the Thirteenth Male Apostle.

'Well, you've found it. Now you can clear off,' shouted the robed figure. Buddy was not scared of this rude person, whoever he was, and walked up the little cobbled path to where he was standing. No one spoke for a few minutes. They both just stood staring at each other. Buddy was rather tubby and stood dressed in his faded blue jeans, white teeshirt and white trainers. Facing him was an Oldie who was tubbier than Buddy and was wearing only a black robe and black shoes. He looked rather strange with nothing between the hem of his robe and his black shoes except two fat white hairy legs.

'I have an appointment with Canon Blast,' said Buddy quietly.

'Not dressed like that you haven't,' replied the person in the doorway. 'I am Canon Blast and you have the choice of either coming back when you're properly dressed in a robe, or not bothering to come back at all. I've got enough trouble without weirdos like you giving me more.' With that the canon turned round and walked back into the Ancient Church of the Thirteenth Male Apostle, slamming the old fourteenth-century wooden door behind him.

Buddy walked away from the old building feeling rather sad at the communication breakdown, but also realising why he was called Canon Blast. As he sat down in the warm sunshine on a grassy bank, ignoring the sign 'YOU MUST NOT SIT DOWN ON THIS GRASSY BANK', he heard a faint noise in the distance. As it slowly grew louder, he guessed that it was coming in his direction.

The first sound that he could decipher was the sound of much jingling. This was followed by loud, high-pitched shouting and a sort of chanting. He leapt to his feet and peered down the roadway in the direction of the sounds.

Then it came into view. He could just make out that it was some kind of procession, and as it came steadily closer it reminded him of a March for the Voice which Newchurch regularly did to aggravate the Enemy Superpowers and to put them in their place. But this was very different.

It was led by a tall slim Oldie of the female variety. She was obviously in charge at the head of the procession and she was wheeling a barrow in front of her with the most enormous copy of the Voice's Manual in it that Buddy had ever seen. Her attire caught Buddy's attention as she was wearing a very smart suit, consisting of grey trousers, jacket and waistcoat, and a tie that was louder than the noise she and her followers were making. As Buddy stared, he noticed that all the marchers were female and again all dressed in smart suits with different coloured ties, and most were waving tambourines with coloured ribbons flowing in all different directions, but all very carefully synchronised.

Those who were tambourineless had banners in their hands, which they waved high as they shouted out such statements as:

We are fighting females,
Released, at last set free.
It's time to lock all males up,
Then throw away the key.

The louder they shouted, the more they waved their banners. Buddy couldn't believe his eyes as he read the wording on some of the banners. 'FIRE THE ROTTEN OLD CANON' said one. 'BLAST FROM THE PAST' read another.

Then suddenly the angry parade stopped on the road right outside the Ancient Church of the Thirteenth Male Apostle. 'Sisters' screamed the one with the wheel barrow at the front, 'Stop!' The entourage stopped obediently, as did their shouting and tambourine bashing. Putting her barrow down she screamed in the direction of the wooden door: 'Come out, Blast, you coward. Fight if you have the guts to. We'll show you who's wearing the trousers now.'

Blast appeared through the door followed by about fifty other male Oldies all dressed in black robes, black shoes and white legs. 'Pastor Kitchen,' he yelled back, 'we are not afraid of you. In fact, as you can see we are expecting you. You should have stayed in the kitchen where you and all your rebellious army belong.'

Between the doorway of the church and the road were two tall piles of earth, and after a few further insults were thrown, both leaders shouted, 'Charge!' and the battle began. Pastor Kitchen and the Modern Movement of the Free Sisters' Fellowship leapt onto the mound on the far left, while Canon Blast and the Ancient Church of the Thirteenth Male Apostle took up their position on the mound on the far right. Then the mud began to fly. Both sides proved to be very accurate and certainly knew how to hit a person where it really hurts.

Buddy stood and watched helplessly as serious injuries were being inflicted on both sides. He gazed at the now deserted big black Manual lying face down in the barrow in the middle of the road. He could see there was going to be no let-up, as the battle became even more furious and the mud-slinging seemed like it was going to last for ever.

Sadly he made his way back towards Newchurch and the blood-curdling screams of the attackers and the pain-stricken wails of the wounded slowly disappeared out of earshot.

He felt sick inside as he knew with warfare of this kind there could be no winners; ultimately all would be losers. But the worst losers of all would be those who belonged to neither the Ancient Church of the Thirteenth Male Apostle nor the Modern Movement of the Free Sisters' Fellowship.

Now was the time to send in the Newchurch hit squad.

As all of Newchurch was excitedly awaiting Buddy's return, nobody noticed a thin female Littlekid leave her bedroom with a small bag containing all her worldly possessions. As the sun disappeared and dusk quickly fell she walked through the streets unrecognised and finally left Newchurch. She knew it would be ages before anyone even realised she was no longer around, because everyone had their minds set on far more important things than her.

6

If You Go Down to the Woods . . . Tonight

Dusk never seemed to want to stay around for long. It was almost as though it had an urgent prior engagement which it had to rush off to fulfil. As quickly as it moved on, darkness crept in to take its place. Runaway Forest was never a place that would scare the Littlekids of Newchurch, though of course they had been taught to be sensible and not to wander alone there after dark, as that could be asking for trouble.

Angela wasn't asking for trouble as she entered the creepy darkness of Runaway Forest. She wasn't asking for anything. When you're running away from yourself, being logical and sensible is the last thing on your mind. Fortunately, the moon had decided to shed a bit of light that night and she was able to see dimly the narrow muddy path that led into the heart of the woods. Small, inquisitive, nocturnal, furry animals ran to the edge of the path to see who was invading their territory, while the wise old owls just hooted and peered down with their large eyes wide open, wondering who would be unwise enough to be walking out alone at this late hour.

Angela shivered as she walked through the freezing night air, her thin coat no competition against the might of the weather. Ahead of her she saw an old tree stump, and feeling tired she decided to rest. Weary, she sat down.

Then she heard it.

It was louder than the owl's hooting and the other small animal noises. It was a crashing, crunching sound and was coming from a distance behind her. It sounded like horses' hooves galloping through the bracken and thick undergrowth, and as the scary sound increased in volume by the second, she knew that whatever it was, it was heading in her direction.

Now she did feel frightened. She leapt up from the tree stump and started running as fast as her tired legs could manage down the path and deeper into the forest, but with every step it sounded like the hooves, and now the snorting of the creature, were not just following her, but were almost upon her. She let out a small cry of terror, but was now out of breath, so only a faint noise escaped her tired lungs. She dare not look back. Her heart was beating like a bass drum and as she felt a painful stitch strike her right side, she realised that trying to outrun it was futile. Angela allowed herself to fall head first into the mud and lay motionless on the ground, trying to catch her breath and weeping with fear.

She didn't dare look up as the galloping became a trot then came to a standstill right behind her. A dull thud followed as someone obviously dismounted and raced over to where she was lying helpless. Rough hands grabbed her thin arms and tied them behind her back, then a smelly, dirty piece of cloth was tied tightly over her eyes. Not a word was spoken as Angela felt herself being lifted up and thrown onto the hard wooden floor of what she assummed was some sort of cart. Then came the crack of a whip and she started moving. Within seconds they were in full flight, with Angela rolling about uncontrollably as the charging horse weaved its way along the winding paths of Runaway Forest.

While all this action was taking place, Buddy had arrived back in Newchurch and, having called an emergency meeting with the excited Hearthunter and Miraclekid, was explaining to them his discoveries in Religios-city.

Many miles away Little Chris was lying in his luxury four-poster bed, dressed in his silk pyjamas, proudly watching the video of that day's programme for the fifth time.

Eventually the horse screeched to a halt. The rider dismounted again and walked over and grabbed hold of a very bruised Angela and tied something tightly around her waist. The next thing Angela knew, she was being hoisted up into the air. Now, Angela was frightened of heights, so she was pleased she was still blindfolded.

Then the upward thrust stopped and for a moment

or two she felt herself dangling in mid-air. She guessed she was a long way off the ground. Again rough hands grabbed her and after carrying her a short distance threw her onto something reasonably soft, but Angela's head cracked against a wooden wall and she fainted.

'Wake up!' yelled a fierce voice. 'You heard me, wake up!' it repeated. Angela felt very dazed as she tried to open her eyes. She also felt very sick from not having eaten for a long time. She felt ice-cold water being poured over her head, which ran down the inside of her teeshirt and made her jump as though she'd received an electrical shock.

Her eyes opened. She was relieved that at least the smelly blindfold and cutting ropes that had held her arms so tightly had been taken away. By the light of a flickering candle she realised that she was in a small wooden cabin and was staring straight into the dirty face of a female Littlekid. Her captor was a bit older and taller than she was and had long black greasy hair. Her body was covered in furs and her arms were bulging with muscles.

'What are you staring at, squirt?' asked the Littlekid rudely, displaying blackened teeth that looked like they had never been introduced to a toothbrush. 'Ain't you ever seen a real body before?'

At this the Littlekid laughed as she poked Angela's skinny body with a filthy finger and even filthier fingernail. 'You were easy to find in the woods,' she continued. 'I could hear your bones rattling a mile off.'

After a few more cruel comments about Angela she picked up some raw vegetables and started to eat them.

Angela continued to look round the sparsely-furnished wooden shack. Apart from the table, chair and the old mattress she was lying on, there was a bed, a small, old-fashioned wood-burning stove, and a photo of two parents and a tiny Littlekid hanging on the wall.

'Yeah, that's me,' said the fur-clad female, seeing that Angela's eyes were gazing at the photo. 'And I think the two Oldies are my mum and dad, but I can't be sure, 'cos I haven't seen them for years. My name's Yolander and you are my prisoner.' She threw a raw potato over to Angela to eat. 'Yolander Onmyturf. Get it?' she grinned. 'Yolander Onmyturf . . . and you're in big trouble. And Littlekid,' she said, getting up from the table and staring at Angela, 'believe me, I ain't kiddin', you are in big trouble.

'Now let's have a look in your bag and see if you have any goodies that might interest me. Hello, what's this?' said Yolander, picking out the photograph of Angela and a male Littlekid that Angela treasured so much. Yolander walked closer to Angela. 'Wow, I guess this used to be you,' she commented. 'But who is this gorgeous hunk of male flesh with you?'

Angela opened her mouth, but found it painful to answer. ''Is name is Little Christian,' she whispered in her broad cockney accent.

'Well, you don't mind if I keep it, do you?' said Yolander loudly. 'I haven't got many pics on my walls as you can see, and this handsome Littlekid will make a great pin-up.' Then, smashing the glass, she took the photo out of its frame. 'Well, I don't need this bit,' she mumbled, tearing the photo in two. She screwed the picture of Angela up and threw it on the floor. 'No offence,' she laughed, 'But I don't want your picture—just his.'

Angela didn't have the strength to argue, but she

winced as she saw her last reminder of the great old days destroyed before her very eyes. It was as if Yolander had pierced her heart with a sharp knife.

Angela grew frightened again. 'Are yer gonna snuff me?' she asked.

'Not unless you give me any trouble,' replied Yolander. 'Anyway, looking at the state of you it seems like you've made quite a good job of trying to kill yourself.'

Angela blushed and felt guilty.

'Now, I'm going to sleep, and if you know what's good for you, I suggest you do the same,' said Yolander after she had pinned Little Christian's photo over her bed. Then she blew out the candle and got under the bedclothes. 'You've got a busy day tomorrow, Littlekid.'

Within minutes Yolander was snoring more loudly than the fearful snorting horse that had been chasing Angela, and although she was tired, she couldn't sleep. 'I must escape,' she thought. 'This evil Littlekid obviously has somethin' awful planned for me and I'm not goin' to wait around to find out what it is.'

Although the room was very dark, the moonlight shone in around the frame of the badly-made door. Quietly, Angela put one leg out of bed. 'If I can make it to the door, I'll be able to make a run for it,' she thought. Then she put her other leg on the floor, but to her horror the potato that Yolander had thrown over to her rolled off the bed and landed with a loud thumping noise on the bare wooden floorboards. 'What's that?' shouted Yolander, but she said it in her sleep and straightaway rolled over and faced the opposite direction and started snoring again.

Angela crept across the floor, hoping that the door facing her would not be locked. Moving at what seemed like an inch a minute she eventually reached it and breathed a short sigh of relief. Then she stretched her thin right arm up to the door catch and very gently eased it upwards. 'Brilliant!' she thought, almost forgetting where she was and wanting to shout for joy. The door wasn't locked.

Slowly standing upright, she opened the door just a fraction, trying to let as little light in as possible. The snoring continued. Then she crept through it and quietly closed it behind her, realising it would be suicide to try and retrieve her bag, or the picture of Little Christian.

Her heart was now racing with excitement. 'I've made it,' she thought. 'I'm free.' Turning away from the door she was just about to make a run for it, when suddenly she halted dead in her tracks. Her face went white as all the blood seemed to drain out of it. Facing her were just branches and dark nothingness. Daring for just a moment to look down she realised it was a sheer drop of about fifty metres to the path below. She was imprisoned in a tree house.

In the past Angela had not been afraid of heights. In fact she hadn't been afraid of anything much, but since she had stopped following the Voice all sorts of fears had taken hold of her.

She glanced briefly down again and felt dizzy. Though still freezing she started to perspire. 'What can I do?' she thought. 'If I go back in the hut I know somethin' 'orrible is going to happen to me. Oh crumbs!' Deep down, even though she was panicking, she knew she had no choice. She must overcome her fear, and escape. Glancing around she saw on her left-hand side a rope-ladder tied to a strong branch. 'It's the only way,' she thought to herself, and mustering all the courage that was left in her she reached out, grabbed it, and closing her eyes started to descend.

Hand over hand, foot over foot, very slowly and all the time trying to stop the ladder from swinging, she climbed down. All of her body was now wet with sweat and her hands were finding it harder and harder to get a firm grip. 'Still, I must be at least halfway,' she thought, still not daring to look below her. Then she froze to the ladder. It was that sound again. Galloping hooves in the distance, charging through the undergrowth and trampling anything that would get in its way. Within seconds she could hear the snorting nostrils just a few metres beneath her. Still she refused to look down.

'So, you prefer my horse Nightmare's company to mine, do you?' screamed an angry voice from the top of the ladder. Angela looked up and saw Yolander staring down at her. 'Well, you have ten seconds to make your choice,' screamed Yolander even more fiendishly. 'Up to Yolander or down to Nightmare.'

As Yolander began to count up to ten, Angela just clung even more tightly to the ladder, now weeping out loud and absolutely petrified. 'Ten!' shouted Yolander and with that pulled out a sharp knife that was tucked away beneath her fur. 'Goodbye, skinny Littlekid,' she yelled as she started cutting the rope on the rope-ladder. 'Enjoy your time with Nightmare.' The nag below was getting highly excitable and as well as snorting even more violently it was menacingly scraping its front right hoof in the mud and frothing at the mouth as though it had gone raving mad.

Angela didn't dare look up or down. As Yolander cut right through one of the ladder ropes, the ladder swung uncontrollably towards the tree. Screaming in desperation Angela shrieked, 'Voice, please 'elp me!' and with that her thin body swung with the ladder and thumped against the mighty tree trunk. Her fingers spontaneously released their grip of the rope, causing her to fall to the darkness below.

7

In None We Trust

It was very early in the morning. A white frost covered the ground of Runaway Forest like a huge white carpet. The horse and cart pulled to a halt. 'I say, have you got me someone?' came the posh voice of the driver.

'Yeah,' came the reply, 'but it ain't much of one I'm afraid; all skinny like.'

'What sort of condition is it in?' said the posh voice.

'Oh, I'm afraid it's a bit roughed up,' came the reply. 'But it's still breathing.'

59

'All right, throw it on the back of my cart, but if it dies within a week you can forget about your pay. Oh, and I almost forgot, Grand Gander is very appreciative of your work and sends his sincere thanks.'

Yolander felt good that her hard work was being appreciated. She lifted the thin body up and placed it in the back of the cart, and without another word being muttered the cart trundled off towards Nochurch.

That same early morning found Little Chris staring at his very expensive, highly-crystalled watch. 'Another five minutes and I must leave,' he thought. He took one last look at himself in his full-length bedroom mirror. Yes, the black shiny patterned suit with the bright yellow tie looked fine, but he put a touch more gel on his hair as he noticed one hair was trying to break free. Perfect.

He left his bedroom and excitedly ran down the stairs, picking up his briefcase as he did so. This was a meeting of a lifetime and he wanted to be sure that he hadn't forgotten anything. Once in the hallway he laid his case on a beautiful antique table and opened it. It contained a portable micro-computer, which contained his diary and would be helpful if he needed to make any notes, a portable micro-cassette recorder—that always came in handy —a pair of shades, a spare handkerchief, a cheque-book, a hair brush, breath mints, a copy of the Voice's Manual and a copy of his latest show on video. 'Yes, I think that's everything,' he considered carefully, but then took out the Manual and left it on the table. 'Perhaps I won't need this today,' he thought on reflection, and with that he closed his case, picked it up and walked out of his front door to the waiting limo.

The sixty-four Gooseys fidgeted nervously as they sat facing the Grand Gander in the now-restored Oddboys' Hall.

'For goodness' sake relax,' shouted their leader, nervously pacing the floor himself. 'This is a great day, for two reasons. The first is that we have an opportunity to meet together twice in one week, and the other is that our dreams have come true. We are about to become a proper sixty-six-member gaggle.'

As Grand Gander moved away from the table, all stared at him noticing that his stomach had expanded since they had last met, but nobody dared say anything. Grand Gander could see that their eyes were aimed at a certain part of his anatomy and simply but embarrassingly explained to them that he was suffering from digestion troubles, which made him look rather larger than usual.

The limo pulled up sharply at the busiest crossroads in Nochurch in the middle of the early morning rush hour and Little Chris stared out of the window at a multicar smash up. The injured and wounded lay everywhere and the noise of exploding vehicles and the people in pain was deafening. It was a horrific scene. As he looked more closely he saw someone dressed in a traffic cop's uniform, waving his hands in all directions, seemingly ignoring the mangled mayhem. Little Chris wound down his electric window and shouted out, 'Oi! What's going on?' At this the uniformed officer stopped waving his arms and marched over towards the limo.

The closer he came, the more Little Chris thought he recognised the face, but even if he didn't, the face obviously recognised him. 'No, it can't be,' shouted the policeman excitedly, now completely ignoring the blood and chaos that continued behind him. 'Yes, it is!' he exclaimed with a huge grin spreading right across his face. 'It's Little Chris, isn't it?'

Little Chris still didn't have a clue who was addressing him, then right in front of his eyes the officer started taking his uniform off, throwing his hat in the air with a yell of glee. 'Well I'll be . . . it's Ron Guidance,' shouted Little Chris in utter amazement, recognising the Oldie with his grey hair and his grey moustache.

'Of course it is,' replied a beaming Ron dumping the uniform on the floor. 'Who did you think it was? Robocop?' And with that he burst out laughing. 'I say, old friend,' he said amid his guffawing, 'we have done well for ourselves, haven't we?' He gazed at all the riches surrounding Little Chris. 'Now be a good chap and give me a lift away from here. You see, all this racket behind me is starting to bring on one of my migraines. I was only given this job this morning because everybody knows how brilliant I am at helping people find direction, but obviously my gifting does not include directing car drivers.'

Little Chris trusted no one, especially so-called old friends. 'But you can't just resign and walk away from this tragic mess,' he said. 'Just think of me for a moment and of my reputation as a TV star. If my fans discovered that I had not only left the scene of a disaster without giving assistance, but also gave a lift to the person who caused it, my viewing figures would be halved and I would be financially finished. Anyway, I have a very important, very private meeting that I must attend and if we don't leave right away I will be late.'

'But you owe me,' said angry Ron. The smile was now gone. 'I helped make you what you are today. It was I who advised you that you didn't need Newchurch any longer.'

'I owe you nothing,' snapped Little Chris just as angrily. 'All you scroungers want to share in my hard-earned success. Listen hard,' he continued, 'I would still be where I am today if I'd never met you. I achieved all I have today by myself and with the help of no one. Now clear off! I hope I never see you again.'

With that Little Chris closed his window and thumped his chauffeur's seat, indicating to him to drive on.

'You wait,' snarled Ron Guidance. 'I'll get even with you, Little Chris, if it's the last thing I do.' And he ran off in the opposite direction to the noise.

While Little Chris and Ron Guidance had been arguing, only one person had been doing something constructive. Sam Ariton, who hated cars and was president of the Prosecute All Polluting Vehicles Movement, had phoned for ambulances and was racing around doing all he could to help those in pain.

'Well, where is he?' grumbled Grand Gander looking at his watch impatiently for the sixth time. 'He is six seconds late and I hate being kept waiting.' This was the cue for all the other Gooseys to look at their watches and all make a tutting sound at the same time. Then outside the hall the screech of brakes silenced everyone. Grand Gander signalled to one of the Pecks to peer carefully out of the door to see who it was.

'It's a big limo,' came the reply from the peering Peck. 'And a Littlekid dressed in a smart black shiny suit has just got out and is heading towards us.' While sixty-four Gooseys looked at each other even more nervously, Grand Gander breathed a sigh of relief. 'Excellent,' he whispered to himself. 'Little Christian, you are just about to know how a fly feels when it first makes contact with a spider's web.'

8

Onwards into the Night

Neither Miraclekid nor Hearthunter had known what to say as Buddy had related the sad story of Religios-city. For the next few days they all spent a lot of time talking and listening to the Voice, as this had not been the news they had expected to receive. This was going to be no normal hit. They needed to replan their strategy.

The Voice made it very clear that now was the time to strike, which thrilled Buddy as this had been his suggestion, but both Hearthunter and Miraclekid were no longer quite as enthusiastic as they were clearly about to embark upon a mission that was unlike anything they had ever experienced.

The Voice also told them that he wanted them to leave in the evening, which would mean that they would arrive in Religios-city under the cloak of darkness and be less conspicuous.

Buddy was thrilled at the turnout of Newchurch to pray over Hearthunter, Miraclekid, Ivor Future, Joy Atalltimes and Hope Itgoeswell (otherwise known as the Fearless Five) before they set off to Religios-city. Like any good Flockwatcher he also made a mental note of those who were not there. Some where obviously looking after their tiny Littlekids, others were feeling unwell, even after being prayed for, and just one or two were probably being a bit rebellious. Buddy turned to Harmony, who was also an excellent Flockwatcher, and asked if she could just pop over and ask Angela to join them. As he wasn't sure if anyone had seen her for the last few days, she might not have known that the meeting was being held.

Harmony quietly slipped out of the meeting room and ran to the small house where Angela had been staying. She went as quickly as she could because she hated missing out on the good-bye prayers. She was about to ring the door-bell, but then she noticed that there were no lights on in the house. 'She must be asleep,' Harmony thought, and looking up at the bedroom window she saw that the curtains were open, but again no sign of any light. This did not seem unusual though to Harmony, as she knew that Angela always slept with the curtains open.

Harmony raced back to the meeting room and discretely pushed her way to the front. 'All her lights are off. She must be fast asleep,' she whispered to Buddy.

'Oh well,' he said, 'probably the best thing, feeling as she does.' But there was disappointment in his voice.

Although Hearthunter and Miraclekid didn't say anything, they were even more disappointed than Buddy by Angela's absence—not so much that she wasn't praying for them, more that she wasn't up to going with them. They had not been on one hit where both she and Little Christian hadn't come into their minds, but they never talked about it; it was still too painful.

The moon had decided not to bother to come out on this night, so the Fearless Five set off with small packs on their backs, containing all the essentials for a few days, a torch in one hand and their Manuals within easy reach in their pockets.

The night air was as usual bitterly cold, but they felt warm inside as they always did when they were being obedient to the Voice. Soon they reached the entrance to Runaway Forest, and Hope asked if there was any way they could walk round it and not through it, as it did look ever so creepy. The others laughed. 'It will be fine,' Hearthunter said, 'so long as we all stay together. Remember the Voice has commissioned us to do this, so he will look after us.'

Once in the wood Hope realised that she had nothing to be afraid of. In fact it was great fun all holding hands, flashing their torchlights everywhere and singing the Littlekids' marching song at the tops of their voices.

The owls peered down and the little furry animals again came inquisitively to the side of the path. It was strange for them to be disturbed twice within a few days.

As the singing continued Miraclekid suddenly

shouted, 'Stop!' They all stopped instantly and went quiet.

'What is it?' asked Hearthunter, surprised.

'Wait, I think I've seen something.' He shone his torch on the path in front of them where they all saw a horse's hoofprints, followed by cartwheels.

'They are a horse's hoofprints,' said Ivor. 'I'd recognise them anywhere.'

'Yes, I realise that,' said Miraclekid rather impatiently. 'But why have they just appeared? And where have they come from?'

He shone his torch to the side of the path and saw that the bracken and bushes had been flattened. 'There's your answer,' said Hearthunter.

'What's so strange about that?'

'Something inside me says that something's not right. No, I'd go as far as to say that something is very wrong.'

With this he left the others and followed the horse and cart tracks further down the path.

'Oh, I'm getting scared,' said Hope and Joy both at the same time.

'And I don't feel so brave either,' remarked Ivor.

Hearthunter shouted after Miraclekid. 'Hey,' he said, 'go easy. You're scaring the Littlekids and we haven't even reached the battlefield yet.'

Miraclekid seemed to be ignoring all of them. He had stopped and was kneeling on the frozen muddy path. 'Look at this!' he shouted. They all ran to where he was kneeling. A large area of grass had been flattened and in the mud it was just possible to make out the imprints of clothing. Miraclekid repeated, 'There's something wrong. If I'm not mistaken, not so long ago a Littlekid was lying here. Look over there to the horse and cart tracks.' They all looked to where the beam of his light was shining. The horse had obviously stopped and from then on the cart track marks were deeper. 'Something—or should I say someone—has been picked up and put on the cart.'

'Come off it,' smiled Hearthunter. 'You've been watching too many mystery movies. Someone may have fallen over or been hurt and a passing cart has picked them up and taken care of them. That does happen, you know.'

Miraclekid was not convinced. 'I'm not going to move from this spot until we talk to the Voice about it. I believe the Voice is trying to show us something.'

Hearthunter knew that once Miraclekid felt something there was no changing his mind. He also knew that Miraclekid was very sensitive to what the Voice was saying, and so he agreed.

As they spoke to the Voice, he showed them all that it was no accident that they had spotted the tracks, but the Voice didn't seem to say anything else.

'I must follow the tracks,' said Miraclekid. 'I really feel that's what the Voice wants me to do.'

'Wait a minute,' said Hearthunter. 'We are on a mission. What about Religios-city? Buddy will go mad if he hears you've gone off and done your own thing. You know how impetuous he thinks you are. You must come with us.'

'I can't,' stated Miraclekid dogmatically. 'You four head towards Religios-city and I will catch you up later. It's not that I'm going against Buddy's wishes, it's just that I'm taking a detour to get there.'

Hearthunter knew he was wasting precious time trying to argue with Miraclekid. 'OK,' he said. 'We will meet you there, but do be careful.' And with that they prayed over each other again, then the four continued their singing as they headed along the path towards Religios-city, while Miraclekid left the path to follow the tracks through the undergrowth.

The further Miraclekid walked, the more quiet the singing became until soon it could be heard no more. Now he felt very alone, and he had to remind himself that he wasn't—the Voice was with him.

Although the horse and cart had made a sort of track, it was not a very good one and the brambles seemed to reach out and scratch and grab him as the stinging-nettles left painful little poisonous bumps on any piece of bare skin they could find.

Then he heard a strange sound. It was far off but certainly heading towards him. 'That's better,' he smiled, with not an ounce of fear in him. 'The horse and cart are going to find me, which will save me the effort of having to find them.' He stood boldly in the cold dark night facing towards the oncoming sound, 'Here I am! Come and get me!' he shouted.

Where he was standing, visibility was very bad, not only due to the darkness, but also due to the dense wood around him, and although the crashing noise of the horse and cart was by now extremely loud, indicating that they were very close, he couldn't quite work out how close. Then to his surprise, instead of seeing the expected sight burst out of the nearby bushes, instantly all went silent, deadly silent.

Even the owls and the furry little animals could not be heard. It was as if someone had ordered every living thing to be still or suffer the consequences. Miraclekid could just hear himself breathing rather heavily, as he now became uneasy. He felt he was being watched by evil eyes, but he couldn't work out where they were hiding.

'I know you are there,' shouted Miraclekid. 'Come out and show yourself.' Still no reply. He started to perspire and as he did so the nettle and bramble wounds seemed to hurt all the more. Then he heard a blood-curdling scream, as someone leapt out from behind him. Something hard thumped him on the back of his head, and he slumped to the ground. On this very dark night, someone had switched his lights out.

Although Hearthunter, Ivor, Joy and Hope knew nothing about all this, they did feel the Voice telling them they should wait at the edge of the forest for a while—this would give Miraclekid the chance to catch them up. But as they lay down on the grass in their thick warm clothes, even though the night was cold, their tired eyelids grew heavier and heavier until none of them could keep them open any longer, and in no time they were all fast asleep.

9

The Admission Charge

As Little Chris entered the Oddboys' Hall the Pecks slammed the doors behind him. Little Chris glanced around and saw sixty-five people, none of whom he recognised. He gazed at the top table, where he saw a tall man of average build with a black moustache who he assumed must be in charge.

'Welcome to the Gooseys' gaggle gathering,' said the tall man standing to his feet and making a vague attempt at a smile. 'Perhaps you would be kind enough to go over to that far corner and stand on the wooden box that we have put there especially for you.' Little Chris was escorted by the two Pecks to the box in the corner.

'I would just like to say,' said Little Chris standing on the box, 'that it is a great priv . . . .'

'Shuddup!' snapped Grand Gander cutting him off in the middle of his sentence. 'You will say nothing until you have past our initiation test, unless I ask you to, and even then you ask permission from me, the Grand Gander, before you utter a word.'

Little Chris went silent, while his face blushed a brilliant red.

'Listen carefully,' continued Grand Gander. 'This is a very exclusive secret society where only the elite from Nochurch ever have the opportunity to belong to the Grand Order Of Secretly Evil Yobs, and we have to check you out to see if you are made of the right material.' The other Gooseys nodded in agreement.

'There are four very simple things you must do before you can be one of us. Are you willing to attempt them? You may answer my question.'

'Yes, Grand Gander,' said Little Chris meekly.

'Well, good. First, we have to teach you to keep your mouth shut. All you have to do is to open your mouth and stick your tongue out. The Pecks will then punch a small hole in it with a sterilised instrument. This tiny hole will always be there to remind you that if you ever disclose any of the Gooseys' secrets, the Pecks will make a much bigger hole, by taking your tongue out altogether. The Pecks liked this bit and smiled at each other.

As Little Chris opened his mouth, he saw the Pecks pull a small hole-punching instrument out of a sealed bag, 'Tongue out,' one of them growled. Little Chris hated any sort of pain and gingerly stuck his tongue out just a little way. 'Further,' grunted the other Peck. Then as one grabbed hold of it, snap, the other allowed the puncher to do it's business. Little Chris howled in pain and almost fell off the wooden box, as blood dripped down his chin.

'Oh, come on now!' exclaimed Grand Gander. 'That didn't hurt much, did it? Remember, there is no gain without pain.' All the other Gooseys nodded seriously, each relieved that they had never had to have their tongues punched.

'Secondly, you need to learn to be humble. All Gooseys, except me of course, are here to serve each other. In other words, you are here to serve us,' declared Grand Gander. 'Pecks, bring out the props.' The Pecks brought out a bucket of hot soapy water, and as they did so all the Gooseys removed their flippers. 'Well, what are you waiting for?' asked Grand Gander. 'It's feet-washing time.'

'Permission to speak please,' gurgled Little Chris, as his mouth was still bleeding. 'What do I wash and dry them with?'

Grand Gander looked hard at him and replied, 'That black suit jacket of yours would be ideal to use as a flannel, and those black trousers I'm sure would serve as a towel. Now get on with it.'

Little Chris removed his beautiful suit and started the long, horrible, arduous task, and the nearer he got to the top table, the more smelly the feet seemed to become. He wondered if any of them had ever cleaned between their toes and reckoned that if he had planted seeds there, there was enough dirt to ensure a great harvest.

Finally, feeling exhausted, he washed the Grand Gander's feet which were without doubt the worst of the lot. He was then taken back to the box in the corner.

'Do please put your suit back on,' insisted Grand Gander. 'What would people think if they walked in and saw you dressed in just your shirt and underpants?' Again all the Gooseys nodded, having put their flippers back on after admiring their clean feet, They felt very relieved that they had never been asked to perform such a humiliating task.

Little Chris put on the dirty, stinking, wet jacket and trousers and stared at Grand Gander, waiting for his next command.

'So far so good,' commented Grand Gander. 'You are now halfway through your initiation and already I feel that you are a much better person than when you first arrived.

'The third lesson you need to learn is that you are nothing compared with me. After all, there is only one leader, only one Grand Gander, and that is the one you are now facing. Within the next two hours you have to say some wonderful, nice things about me—which you shouldn't find very hard as of course there are plenty of things to choose from—but alongside those wonderful compliments, I want you to make honest comments about yourself in comparison with me. Give him an example, Bigsby Bankbalance, of what I am talking about.'

Bigsby, who had been dozing off after having a wonderful daydream about counting bank notes, sat up in surprise. 'Er, yes of course, Grand Gander,' he stammered. 'You, Grand Gander,' he continued, 'are rich in every sense of the word, whereas I, with all my worldly fortune, am like a penniless, bankrupt, broke, destitute, impecunious, needy, obolary, poverty-stricken, skint beggar in comparison.'

'Yes, that just about sums you up,' said a very condescending Grand Gander. 'Now, it's your turn, Little Chris.'

Little Chris didn't know where or indeed how to begin. 'Um, you are very good looking and I am not so good looking,' he stammered.

'Rubbish!' screamed Grand Gander, cutting him short as all the gaggle booed and hissed to give him moral support. A Peck cuffed Little Chris round the back of the head.

'I'm sorry,' came a weedy sound from Little Chris's mouth. 'What I meant to say is that you are very good looking and I am very ordinary and plain.'

'Rubbish!' screamed out Grand Gander even more loudly so his voice could be heard over the deafening boos and hisses. The other Peck cuffed him even harder.

'I'm sorry,' wailed Little Chris. 'What I meant to say is that you are the best looking, most attractive, glamorous, handsome, visually stunning, gorgeous person in the world and I am the most ugly, disgusting, revolting, nasty, objectionable piece of nothing ever to crawl out from under a stone.'

'That's much better,' exclaimed Grand Gander with the background ballyhoo now changing from boos to cheers. 'And much more truthful,' he added.

For the following one hour and fifty-five minutes Little Chris smothered Grand Gander with every compliment imaginable, while at the same time putting himself down to depths so low that he actually began to believe not only every honouring observation he made about his new leader, but also every horrible thing that he said about himself.

The two hours were up. Little Chris hardly had the strength to stand on the box. His mouth was still painful, though it had stopped bleeding, his clothes were still damp and had started to steam and smell even worse, and now he had indoctrinated himself into believing that Grand Gander was the greatest thing since the invention of the TV camera and in doing so had not just been humbled, but had allowed every bit of self-worth to be crushed out of him.

The Gooseys looked at each other in amazement, relieved that when it had been their turn they had only had to speak for ten minutes, not two hours. Grand Gander looked at him feeling well pleased with himself. 'Little Chris, so far you have learned three very important lessons. To summarise: the first is that as a Goosey you will be sworn to silence; the second, that as a Goosey you are nobody special—you are just one of the gaggle; thirdly, you have learned that you no longer do what you want to do. You now do what I want you to do.'

Little Chris just managed a nod.

'The final part of your initiation is the most simple. It is quite painless and the only action required is that of your hand giving an autograph. Pecks, help him over here to my table.'

The Pecks almost had to carry him over to where Grand Gander was seated. Grand Gander waved a very official-looking piece of paper in the air. 'We all know that the job you do requires a certain amount of devotion to, ah, now how can I put it without upsetting the rest of the gaggle? I know, to your idea of a superior being,' whispered Grand Gander. 'The final thing you need to do to become one of us,' he continued, 'is to sign your name at the bottom of the Goosey contract of total loyalty and absolute allegiance.'

Little Chris's eyes were very bloodshot and quite bleary, but he could still read the words in front of him.

I, Little Chris, promise that no person (alive or dead) will be more important to me than Grand Gander and the Grand Order Of Secretly Evil Yobs. I am sworn to secrecy and put myself into their hands, committing the rest of my life to them. I understand that if I break this promise, my existence will be terminated.

Signed:

Witness:

Little Chris had hated the initiation ceremony and the humiliating tasks that he had taken part in, but he also knew that if he really wanted to be somebody, he had to be part of this group.

As he read through the contract a second time, he heard a very quiet voice that he had not heard for a long time whispering into his mind the words, 'Don't do it.'

'Whose voice is that?' he thought. 'I don't recognise it.' But it kept saying the same words.

Grand Gander was now getting impatient and had started to perspire. For the first time that day his stomach gave a loud rumble, reminding him it was nearly lunchtime. 'Come on!' he snapped. 'We haven't got all day. What on earth's the matter? You do want to be one of us, don't you?'

Little Chris held the pen tightly. 'Grand Gander,' he said painfully, 'you know I want to join you, but a voice I don't recognise is telling me not to, and it's so powerful it's paralysed my right hand. Look, I can't move it.'

Grand Gander was now in a real panic. 'Listen, Little Chris,' he yelled, 'if you don't sign this you will be finished. No one turns down Grand Gander and lives to be successful.' As he said this he ran around and stood next to Little Chris and held the hand that had the pen in it. 'Now listen carefully, This is your very last chance. I am not going to ask you again,' he murmured with a murderous tone in his voice. 'Answer me. Do you want to sign it?'

Little Chris tried to speak, but now found that his lips had frozen together and he couldn't even open his mouth. But he did manage a slight nod of the head.

'That's all I need to know,' said a relieved Grand Gander, and forcing his hand painfully downwards to where the contract lay on the table he managed to manoeuvre the pen so it wrote a cross. 'Thank you,' smiled Grand Gander, snatching the contract and signing his own name next to the word 'witness'. He put it safely into his pocket. 'That is all I needed. At last,' he whispered under his breath, 'I've got you. You now belong to me. Dad, you'll be proud of me.'

He walked back to the head of the table, beaming all over his face. 'All stand!' he shouted. All the gaggle obediently rose. 'With the power invested in me as Grand Gander, I officially welcome Little Chris as our new member. Your uniform will be delivered to your dwelling place within a few days, and seeing the bad physical state you are in we will see that you receive one of the Goosey perks, which I'm sure will help you back to full health. Major, you acquired that last, ahem, servant. Can you see that he or she is delivered very quickly to our new associate.' The Major saluted obediently. 'Now, let's all raise our hands and shake our fists in the air as we sing our immortal anthem,' said Grand Gander.

As Goosey Goosey Gander was released from sixty-five pairs of lungs at full volume, the Pecks too raised their hands and Little Chris slumped to the floor feeling totally exhausted. Yet for the first time in years he finally felt accepted. This had been a morning he would never forget.

The hall emptied and as usual a very contented Grand Gander was the last to leave. As he entered the bright glare of the midday sunshine he heard a *psssst* noise coming from the shadow at the side of the building. He walked over to where the sound had come from and he could just make out the shape of a thin Oldie. 'Hello Ron,' said Grand Gander. 'It's nice to see you again.' He handed Ron a brown envelope with his agreed fee and then a small bottle with some pills in it. 'Please see that Little Chris receives these personally. I've a feeling he is going to need them.'

From the shadows, Ron's smiling white teeth stayed clenched as he replied, 'It will be my pleasure.'

Without anything else being said, the men parted company.

IO

Nothing Goes to Plan

'I don't believe it!' yelled a frantic Hearthunter staring at his watch. 'It's midday. We must have been asleep for hours.' The other three Littlekids were rubbing their eyes in disbelief. 'But we only put our heads down for a short doze,' said Ivor Future as the bright, warm midday sun was making it very hard to open and focus his eyes.

'What shall we do now?' asked Hope Itgoeswell. 'I remember Buddy saying that we should enter Religios-city at night.'

'I know,' frowned Hearthunter. 'You've no need to remind me.'

'I wonder where Miraclekid is,' said Joy Atalltimes, not wanting to be left out of the conversation.

'Oh, knowing him,' said Hearthunter, 'he will be in the middle of Religios-city doing all sorts of wonderful things. He will probably complete the mission before we even get there.'

'So we are going to hit it in the daylight, are we?' enquired Hope.

'We have no choice. I know Buddy will be mad at me, but what else can we do? And we still have a long walk before us,' groaned Hearthunter. 'Come on, we'd better get going.'

None of them really felt like singing any more. They just hoped they were doing the right thing.

Miraclekid ached all over and was very bored just sitting tied up in a sparsely-furnished wooden hut all morning. He had asked the Voice to burn through the rope for him so he could escape, but the Voice had told him just to wait and be patient, which were the two things he most hated doing. As he waited he gazed for the umpteenth time around his gloomy prison. 'This is very untidy,' he thought. 'Whoever lives here hasn't even bothered to make the bed.' It was as he looked at the blanket on the bed that his eyes glimpsed a torn photo above it. It was too dark to see who was in the photo so he rolled over on the floor to get a better look. Suddenly he realised who it was. 'There is only one person I know who would be carrying that photo around with them,' he said out loud. 'And I thought Angela was back in Newchurch. She must be lost—and I'm on the trail that will lead to her!'

Then he heard the faint noise of the horse and

cart, and when that had stopped he heard a sort of creaking. The door burst open and he came face to face with Yolander Onmyturf.

'Hi!' said Miraclekid as cheerfully as he could manage in his painful situation. 'Wow! You must be strong for a Littlekid,' he said looking at her. 'You've certainly got the drop on me.'

'No one is stronger than me,' replied Yolander. 'You male Littlekids think you're so tough and we females are just weak little things. Well, I'm out to prove you all wrong.'

'Hold your horses,' shouted Miraclekid, suddenly realising that this was a very apt comment after the night before. 'I'm not just any ordinary Littlekid. I'm one of the Children of the Voice and I believe female Littlekids are as important and special as we males.'

'I don't believe you!' screeched Yolander. 'All you males are the same and I don't trust any of you. Mind you, I don't trust females either.'

'Well anyway, have you seen anyone around here lately?' asked Miraclekid, trying to change the subject. 'A skinny female Littlekid for instance, who is probably a bit younger than yourself?'

'Nope,' said Yolander. 'The only ones who live in this forest are me and Nightmare my horse.'

'Well, who gave you that picture of that male Littlekid stuck above your bed?' enquired Miraclekid further.

'Mind your own business,' shouted Yolander getting angry again. 'If any Littlekids like you stray into the Runaway Forest at night it is my job to capture them. I have my orders.'

'And who gives you these orders?' asked Miraclekid.

'Mind your own business,' shouted Yolander again. 'You really are a nosey Littlekid, aren't you.'

'One last question,' said Miraclekid seeing that he was getting nowhere. 'What are you going to do with me now you have captured me?'

'The same as I've done with all the rest,' replied Yolander, calming down a bit. 'I'm going to sell you to the Gooseys of Nochurch who will make you one of their slaves.'

'The Gooseys in Nochurch,' said Miraclekid looking alarmed and for the first time a little frightened. 'I've heard about them, and the Littlekid slave-trade they're mixed up in. I've also heard that once in the hands of the Gooseys the Littlekids are never seen again. Rumour has it that the strong ones are sent to faraway lands, while the weak . . . are killed.'

'I haven't got a clue what they do with them,' said Yolander. 'And it's none of my business. They pay me to give them Littlekids and that's all I know and that's all I want to know.'

'But you wouldn't hand me over to them, would you?' pleaded Miraclekid. 'After all, I could be your friend.'

'I don't need any friends. I didn't even need any family. They always end up leaving you,' said Yolander, now quietly.

Miraclekid could see that this was one hurt Littlekid and the Voice was encouraging her to share some of her hurts.

'Listen,' said Miraclekid gently, 'why don't you tell me your name and how you got to be working for the Gooseys.'

Yolander sat down next to Miraclekid. 'My name is Yolander Onmyturf,' said Yolander. 'I was born in Nochurch and when I was only a tiny Littlekid my mum ran off with another male Oldie. It was soon after that on one dark night that my dad, wanting to get rid of me, brought me here to Runaway Forest and left me alone to die. Although at first I was very frightened,' she continued, shivering at the memory, 'and really thought I was a gonner, it was then a miracle happened. A tall thin Oldie riding on a horse appeared, and although he never smiled he picked me up and rode into the heart of the forest until we reached this house. "This will be a nice place for you to live," said the Oldie. "And here, you can have my horse Nightmare as a gift."

'Although I never saw the Oldie again,' she proceeded, 'food would always appear and then as I grew older so did the demands. Notes were pinned to my tree saying things like, "I saved your life, now you owe me one. All you have to do is capture any Littlekids found wandering in the forest at night, then hand them over to one of my Goosey friends and I will pay you well," and the notes were signed "GG."'

'Grand Gander himself,' mumbled Miraclekid disgustedly.

'So,' ended Yolander, 'now you know it all.' Suddenly she realised that for the first time ever she had made herself vulnerable by sharing her life story. What on earth made her do it, and to an unknown male Littlekid as well? She now felt embarrassed and leapt up and walked away from Miraclekid towards her unmade bed. Then she ripped the photo of Little Christian off the wall and tore it into tiny pieces. 'See, I don't need anyone,' she growled viciously. Miraclekid was a bit worried and asked the Voice what he should do now, but the Voice just continued to say, 'Wait and be patient.'

Suddenly Miraclekid had an idea, which unfortunately was not part of the Voice's plan.

'Yolander,' said Miraclekid, 'who do you think is the stronger—you or me?'

Yolander made a huffing sound and flexing her impressive muscles snarled, 'I am, of course.'

'Rubbish!' exclaimed Miraclekid. 'I have the Voice on my side and together we could dispatch you into the middle of the next century.' Yolander didn't like this sort of talk, as she believed the only thing that she had in life of any value was her strength.

'Listen,' continued Miraclekid, 'I challenge you in combat. If I win, I go free. If you win, I will go quietly with the Goosey slave-traders.'

Yolander could not refuse the chance to show off her strength, so she nodded. She then took a knife from inside her fur and walked towards Miraclekid. 'Hey, no knives,' he shouted. 'Hand-to-hand combat was what I was thinking of.'

Yolander half-smiled as she cut the ropes that were binding Miraclekid. 'Follow me,' she said, 'and don't try to run away because Nightmare is even less friendly than I am.'

'Impossible,' smiled a relieved Miraclekid, rubbing his wrists, pleased that the rope had been taken off. Obediently he followed her to the wooden door. Miraclekid was surprised that they were stuck up in a tree, but seeing the rope-ladder and being very fit himself he had no trouble following Yolander down it.

As he neared the bottom of the ladder he heard those galloping hooves again, but when Yolander shouted, 'Stay,' Nightmare stopped in his tracks like an obedient, well-trained puppy.

Once on the ground they faced each other. 'I'm going to show you once and for all that female Littlekids can be stronger than male ones,' yelled Yolander.

'You haven't got a chance against me and the Voice,' shouted a triumphant Miraclekid very confidently.

As Yolander came flying towards him with her fists clenched he shouted, 'I command you to stop in the name of the Voice.'

But she didn't and the fist thumped him so hard that he lost his balance and fell over. Yolander continued to make mincemeat of him, while Miraclekid kept shouting everything from, 'Fists, be still!' to, 'Eyes, go blind!'. Eventually Yolander got off him as he lay in a moaning heap. He'd not only lost the fight, but he'd also lost his voice with all the shouting.

'If you'd stopped shouting and started fighting you may have done better,' observed the gloating and victorious Yolander.

It was then that another horse and cart arrived. 'Apologies for being a bit late, but we had a very important meeting and then I had a few things I had to attend to at the bank before I could get here,' said the voice on the cart.

'No problem,' said Yolander. 'I'll put your latest acquisition on the cart. There won't be any need to tie him up. This one's all mouth and no muscle.'

'Oh dear, he's in a bit of a mess,' said the voice on the cart as Yolander threw Miraclekid onto the wagon.

'He'll live,' said Yolander. 'And I'll be in to the bank to get my money tomorrow.' By the way, is that skinny female Littlekid I gave to the Major still alive?' she asked.

'Yes,' came the voice from the cart. 'The Major said that she is just about alive, but I wouldn't go racing to him for your wages, because it looks unlikely that she will last the week.'

With this the horse and cart and the badly beaten-up and very disillusioned Miraclekid left Runaway Forest.

As Yolander climbed back up the ladder and sat on a branch in the warm sunlight she felt a strange feeling. She didn't recognise it because she had never felt it before. She kept thinking about Miraclekid. He was different from all the others. She'd actually had a real conversation with him, and even though he did keep shouting strange things about the Voice, he had more courage than anyone else she ever captured. 'I wonder if this is the feeling you get when you make a friend,' she pondered.

As she continued thinking, she suddenly felt sick and bad inside. Something in her head was telling her that she should have let him go. Something in her mind was telling her that he was heading for great danger. And it was all her fault.

II

A Death and Life Situation

It was late afternoon when Hearthunter, Hope,
Ivor and Joy approached the outskirts of Religios-
city. The sun had fallen slightly, but was still
providing plenty of light and warmth. They were
surprised when they saw a sign saying: 'YOU ARE
NOT WELCOME IN RELIGIOS-CITY UNLESS
YOU OBEY OUR RULES' laying on the ground—
not standing upright as it obviously should have
been. It looked like someone had disagreed with
it, uprooted it and thrown it down in disgust.
'Well,' said Hearthunter smiling, 'it sure looks like

Miraclekid has beaten us here. He always tends to leave a trail of destruction behind him. Now, quickly, follow me.'

All four hid behind a broken stone wall while Hearthunter started sharing his strategy for attack. 'We could creep in and try not to be noticed and gradually infiltrate the people by knocking on their doors this evening, but I think that would be wasting even more precious time. My suggestion is that we just walk in very confidently singing the Littlekids' Marching Song and I'm sure we will find that Miraclekid has prepared the way for us, so it should be easy.'

His three young listeners nodded in agreement.

They stepped out from behind the safety of the wall and Hearthunter positioned them in a line. 'I will go on the left, then Joy will stand next to me. Hope, you stand next to Joy and Ivor you will stand on the right.' All did as they were told. 'Now on my command of march, we will head towards the main street and not stop singing till I say so. March!'

As the eight feet started marching, so the four voices starting singing.

There is no one else around
In the air, or on the ground,
Who has the power, has the power of the Voice.
So you Enemy Superpowers,
In your defeated final hours,
We command you to leave, you have no choice
(you have no choice)
As we speak in the authority of the Voice.

So the four heroes entered Religios-city, but as they reached the main shopping centre they couldn't believe their eyes. It was as if they had just entered a riot zone. Tons of wooden signs and masses of smart clothing were burning on a large bonfire in the middle of the street, and the people were yelling and cheering every time another sign or suit was thrown into the blazing flames. Hearthunter, Joy, Hope and Ivor continued their marching and singing, although the marching was noticeably slower and the singing was considerably quieter and less tuneful.

It was then that a Littlekid who was standing by the fire turned and saw them and above the bedlam jumped up and down screaming at the crowd and pointing in their direction.

Things went quiet as angry faces turned away from the fire and stared at the four Children of the Voice. The mob looked very scruffy and untidy. All ages, from tiny Littlekids to Oldies, were present. Hearthunter told his Littlekids to stop singing and walking. Only the crackling of the blazing fire could be heard.

Nobody said anything for several moments. Both sides just stared at each other, wondering who was going to say or do something first. It was a tall Oldie who broke the silence. 'Who are you and what do you want with us?' he yelled.

'We are from Newchurch,' shouted back Hearthunter boldly, 'and we have come to tell you about the Voice.'

The crowd looked round at each other and started whispering.

'Do you have the same beliefs as Canon Blast and Pastor Kitchen?' shouted a young female voice this time.

'Well,' replied Hearthunter truthfully, 'having met neither of these people I am not sure, because I've never talked to the Canon or the Pastor to find out what they really do believe.'

'Well I think you should meet them,' shouted the Oldie who had spoken to them first. 'Get 'em, lads, and let's give them a formal introduction.'

The next thing that Hearthunter, Joy, Hope and Ivor knew was that they were roughly grabbed and their arms painfully forced up their backs. 'Have no fear,' Hearthunter shouted, 'the Voice is with us.' But his voice was by now very shaken and it did not instil a whole heap of confidence in his three junior friends.

The large crowd walked a short distance then stopped opposite what Hearthunter presumed must be the Ancient Church of the Thirteenth Male Apostle.

All went quiet again. Hearthunter was dragged through the church gate by the gang spokesman and stopped a short distance from the large doors. 'Let me introduce you to Canon Blast and Pastor Kitchen,' said the Oldie who still had a tight grip on his arm.

Hearthunter stared at the doors, expecting them to appear. 'I think you're looking for them in the wrong direction. Try looking to your right and down a bit.'

Hearthunter couldn't believe his eyes as he found himself staring at a very large new gravestone. His captor allowed him to go free as he walked over to read the inscription upon it.

Here lie Canon Blast and Pastor Kitchen,
  Otherwise known as the 'you must nots'.
  They made everyone's lives miserable when they were alive.

*May they continue to make each other's lives
miserable now they are dead.*
They won't R.I.P.

Hearthunter was lost for words, but just managed
to ask what had happened.

'They tried to make all us ordinary non-religious
people live under their religious laws,' shouted a
voice from the crowd. 'They told us what we could
and couldn't do— even what clothes we must wear.
They made living unbearable.'

'Yeah, and they never stopped warring between
themselves,' shouted another, 'and finally the
inevitable happened: they destroyed each other and
also their poor confused followers.'

'So we won't allow Newchurch to bring in another
set of rules,' said the Oldie, who had grabbed hold
of Hearthunter's arm again. 'From now on there
will be no religious laws and no religiosity. We
will all believe what we choose to believe.' All the
crowd cheered in agreement.

'Wait, you're right,' shouted Hearthunter, pulling
himself free and leaping up onto a wall. At this point
Ivor, Joy and Hope all knew he was now getting
very excited and was about to launch into a full-scale
attack.

'We are not here to bring you religious laws
which end up like chains and imprison you. We
are here to tell you that the Voice came to earth
and gave his life to set captives free. Look at us:
no suits, and Littlekids who are full of fun. Can
you see any similarity between us and Blast and
Kitchen?'

He heard the crowd whispering 'no' to each other,
which fired him up all the more.

'We will never force you to do anything, I promise. All we want is the chance to tell you about the love the Voice has for you, then leave you to make up your own minds whether you want to be Voice-followers or not. It will be your choice, not our laws.'

The crowd looked at each other, not sure what to think.

'Listen,' pleaded Hearthunter, 'to prove that we are genuine we will help you break down and burn all the "YOU MUST NOT" signs. We hate them as much as you do.'

This was just the proof the crowd needed. Although some were still uneasy about the Voice followers, others invited them into their homes to discuss things further.

12

What a Way to Go

Rhoda Skateboard had been feeling a bit fed up. It seemed that while all her best friends had been invited to take part in different adventures for the Voice, she had been left back at Newchurch where the only action taking place was Buddy updating his graph each day.

She had been to have a chat with Buddy, but the most audacious thing that he had offered to break her boredom was to deliver some of his letters on her skateboard. She reluctantly agreed and set off with her pile of letters. 'Oh well,' she thought, 'my first responsibility was to be a postwoman, and here I am back in the same job.' As she rode her skateboard to the first house, she allowed her mind to drift back to that first letter she had delivered. It had been a commission sent from the Voice's Training Module to Little Christian, who was at that time the leader of Newchurch. She missed Little Christian. He had been quite a tough leader, but she still had great respect for him.

She pushed the first envelope through the appropriate letter box and then looked at the following one to see where her next destination was. It was for Angela. Back on her skateboard, her memory started working overtime and she remembered arriving in Little Christian's office and seeing a photo of Little Christian and Angela. They both looked so happy, and if she hadn't known better she would have thought that they were in love.

Rhoda knew that Angela was in a bad way—well, everyone did—and realising that she hadn't seen her for a long time she decided not just to push the letter through the letter box, but to ring the bell and give it to her in person. She might like to have a female chat, even though Rhoda knew Angela was a lot older and would probably not want to talk much to her. The bell rang, but there was no answer. She rang it again and looked up at the window. The curtains were open.

'She must be in. Everyone knows Angela never goes out.' Rhoda plucked up courage and tried the door handle. The door opened. She shouted up the stairs: 'Angela!' but there was no reply. Quietly she crept up the stairs, and as the bedroom door was open she peered in. 'Wow!' thought Rhoda in surprise as she rushed into the room. 'She's gone!'

Rhoda knew that Angela didn't possess a lot, but she could see that her clothes' drawers were empty and her coat was missing. She almost fell down the stairs. There wasn't a minute to lose. It was full speed on her skateboard back to Buddy's office where she literally fell in through his door.

'Angela's gone!' she gasped breathlessly.

Buddy leapt up. 'Gone where?' he asked.

'How should I know?' said Rhoda. 'All I know is that all her things have gone from her house.'

'There's no time to lose. Follow me,' said Buddy, looking worried. They made their way as quickly as they could back to the house to see if she had left any clues. There was nothing except a stale smell which indicated that the windows hadn't been opened for quite a time.

'Pack some warm clothes, Rhoda. We're going to find her. I am a Flockwatcher and if any Littlekid wanders off, it is my responsibility to search for them until I find them.'

Buddy told Harmony to get Newchurch praying and left her in charge. 'We will head for Religios-city first to see if she joined the Miraclekid and Hearthunter hit squad. I'm hoping that is where she will be.'

Within a very short time Buddy and Rhoda were walking briskly through Runaway Forest. 'It shouldn't take us too long at this pace,' said Buddy striding out, but already Rhoda had a stitch. She was not used to walking. It was always easier to skateboard everywhere—except maybe on a grass path through a forest.

'Well, Junior, I'm glad you managed to drop in for a few days,' said Greedy Gutrot smiling all over his obese face. 'It's always nice to see you, but it's even nicer when you bring me such good news about the biggest pain of my career, Little Christian.' That last name was more spat than spoken by the old arch-enemy of the Children of the Voice. Junior was pleased that he had done something to please his father. His upbringing had not been a very happy one, as the whole family had argued and fought every minute of the day.

'Well, Father, the minute I found I'd achieved something that you never managed to achieve I just had to come and see you. You may be a big fat failure, but it must please you to know that your son is a success.'

'Don't push it, Junior,' snapped Gutrot. 'I've had Little Christian in the palm of my hands before. I suggest you don't count your chickens yet. He's a slippery, slimy, cool customer.'

'Correction, Father, he was, but that was in your day. Now he's a blubbering mess who has given himself over to my control—and I have the contract to prove it. I can destroy him anytime I like.'

'Well do it straightaway, fool. Don't play games with him—he's dangerous.'

'Don't you tell me what to do, fatso. I'll destroy him when I choose and not when you tell me to . . . .'

And so the arguing continued. Happy days were here again.

'By the way,' said Greedy Gutrot in a pause between fights, 'I'm glad to see you've managed to put on some weight. You're looking more and more like your old dad every time I see you.'

'Pig off,' snarled Junior, and the arguments continued.

Back in Nochurch, life had taken a turn for the worse for Little Chris. His health had gone steadily downhill since becoming a Goosey. Every television appearance he made became more pathetic—not helped by the fact that the hole in his tongue meant he couldn't even speak properly. Each failure became a more successful failure than the last.

'What on earth has happened to you, lovey?' wailed Hugo Yourway. 'Your charisma has left you, your viewing audience has deserted you, and now Sativision have told me I have to fire you. I thought we had a future together, but the way you're looking and sounding, Chrissy darling, I don't think you have a future—certainly not in television.'

Little Chris left the studios for the last time, without saying a word. It seemed like he'd managed to become a Goosey, but lost everything else. He had never known such depression as he was experiencing now.

'Wait a minute, Little Chris,' came a familiar voice just as he was about to crawl into his car. He turned and saw Ron Guidance smiling at him. 'Hey, no hard feelings,' he said. 'I'm sorry about the little argument we had last time we met at the pile-up in town. I was a bit upset and didn't mean what I said.'

Little Chris didn't say a word. He just nodded sadly as he sat in the back seat staring blankly downwards. 'Listen,' said Ron in a comforting tone, 'you look bad and Ron is always good at directing people to an exciting future, however bad they may look. Have you ever seriously thought,' he continued, 'that perhaps your future good times are not here on earth? Perhaps you would be happier if you ended it all.'

Little Chris had never contemplated suicide

before, but then he had never ever felt this low. He continued to look at the floor of the car and nodded. Ron pushed a bottle of pills into Little Chris's hand. 'Take these when you get home. All the best in your future life.' Ron shut the door and walked off, rubbing his hands together and smiling. 'Good-bye and good riddance,' he whispered under his breath.

On reaching his home Little Chris almost fell out of his car and staggered up his steps. In his hallway were still plenty of letters, but these were no longer pay cheques and fan mail. They were bills and letters from numerous debt collectors.

He slouched in his chair with an uncorked whole bottle of Sacro Vino in one hand and Ron's pills in the other. He took a swig out of the bottle, then putting it down on the floor he slowly started to unscrew the lid on the pill bottle.

'The Gooseys have destroyed me!' he whispered. 'They have ruined my life.' Then he thought, 'Perhaps I have destroyed myself. I left Newchurch. I could not forgive those who wronged me. Yet I guess they were the only ones who really loved me. I told the Voice what I was going to do for him instead of listening to what he wanted to do with me. A Little Christian living in Nochurch is a contradiction in terms. I've fallen too far to be rescued. Voice, please forgive me. I really am sorry.'

He tipped a handful of pills into his hand and opened his mouth.

Suddenly the door-bell rang and a voice shouted, 'Two gifts for Little Chris—special delivery.'

'Leave them inside the front door,' Little Chris whimpered pathetically, but just loud enough for the delivery Oldie to hear. The door opened and he heard something soft, then something heavier, fall onto the floor before the door slammed shut.

Holding the pills in his hand he slowly made his way into the hall. 'What the . . .' he exclaimed as the pills fell from his hand and bounced all over the wooden floor. There in front of him were two packages. The small one was obviously his new Goosey gear (he could make out the shape of the flippers), but the larger one was a body wrapped in brown paper. He ran over to the body and read the label which said: 'Your very own personal slave, with love from the Gooseys.'

He could see that the body was breathing, but with the brown paper covering the face he was scared stiff that it was about to suffocate. He carefully tore the paper covering the mouth and nose, then ripped it a bit higher to reveal two eyes wide open and staring at him. Suddenly his whole body went numb. 'Angela!' he whispered.

'Little Christian, is that really you?' she replied.

13

Going Nowhere . . . Fast

'I can't believe this,' groaned Miraclekid. 'For the
first time in my life I am surrounded by more money
than I ever dreamed existed, yet I can't get out to
spend it.' At that point he heard a few buttons being
pressed and the huge bomb- and bullet-proof door
opened. Bigsby Bankbalance brought in a tray with
a plateful of burgers and fries on it, plus a large diet
cola. 'Well, thanks very much,' said Miraclekid with
genuine appreciation, and started eating.

'Perhaps you could tell me, Mr Bank Manager,
how long I have been locked away in your vault

and how long you are planning to keep me in it?'

Bigsby glared at him and was surprised that he was in such high spirits after all these days. 'The answer is simple, Littlekid. You have been entertained by me for just a couple of days, and in a very short time you will be leaving us and be taken to another country far away.'

'Well,' said Miraclekid smiling, 'I hope it's somewhere hot and you have packed me some swimming gear, because I'm about due for a vacation.'

Bigsby sat on some money bags and had to admit he was fascinated by Miraclekid. 'Why are you so relaxed?' enquired Bigsy.

'Well, no point in getting stressed out, is there?' chuckled Miraclekid. 'I mean, stress is a major cause of many illnesses and I don't want any of them if I'm about to travel to somewhere nice, do I: And anyway,' he added, as an afterthought, 'the Voice is looking after me.'

Bigsby squirmed at that name. 'Well the . . . one you are talking about hasn't done too well so far, has he?' sneered Bigsby. 'I would say you are now in my hands, not his hands, wouldn't you?'

'Well now, that's interesting,' argued Miraclekid, 'cause I thought just for a few seconds when I was losing that fight with Yolander that he had let me down, but then I realised I was trying to tell him what to do, which of course was right out of order, because he wanted me to be here with you.'

Bigsby didn't like that answer and it made him feel very uneasy in the presence of this strange Littlekid. 'Why do you think he wants you here?' asked Bigsby nervously.

'Well,' replied Miraclekid, 'I'm not one hundred

per cent sure, because he hasn't told me yet, but I've got a feeling he is about to destroy the Gooseys. What do you think, Mr Bank Manager?'

Bigsby didn't answer. He got up and walked straight out, locking the vault behind him. He was now very scared of his prisoner.

As Buddy and Rhoda walked past the Religioscity sign lying on the ground, Buddy smiled to himself thinking that Miraclekid had passed this way before.

He was even more surprised when they reached the main shopping area to see that there were no signs or suits, but friendly people. 'I can't believe it,' he whispered to Rhoda. 'The hit squad must have been a devastating success. Everything is the opposite to how it was last time I was here.'

'Hey, Buddy, Rhoda! It's great to see you! What are you doing here?' They looked over by the chemist shop and saw Ivor shouting and waving to them. After hugging each other Buddy asked where the other Littlekids were. 'Well,' said Ivor, 'Hope and Joy are teaching some tiny Littlekids about the Voice in school, and Hearthunter is in the Town Hall, as the people here have allowed us to use one of their rooms to hold our Newchurch meetings.'

'Brilliant!' said Buddy and Rhoda together.

'And where is Miraclekid?' asked Rhoda.

'Oh, he hasn't been here. He left us in Runaway Forest to try and find a horse and cart, and we assumed that he had returned to Newchurch.'

'What?' stormed Buddy. 'He left Hearthunter and you three Littlekids in the middle of Runaway Forest in the middle of the night to go and do his own thing? He will be in trouble next time I see him!

Not only has he been disobedient, but he's also been totally irresponsible.'

'Hey, calm down,' said Ivor. 'All the shoppers are looking at you. I suggest you'd better come and talk it over with Hearthunter.'

They walked a short distance to a modern building which had an attractive sign outside saying 'Town Hall.'

'We meet just in here, through the door on the right,' said Ivor, leading the way into a nice warm bright room with plenty of windows.

'Well, well, Buddy and Rhoda—how great to see you,' came a voice behind the door that happened to belong to Hearthunter.

After a hug Buddy and Rhoda sat down and listened while Ivor made them all a cup of tea and Hearthunter told them the whole story. He explained about the horse and cart in the forest, and how Miraclekid was convinced that the Voice told him that he must go and investigate it, to which Buddy just made an obviously disapproving huffing sound.

He then went on to explain that they hadn't taken the signs down, it was the locals who had done that after the fight to the bitter end between Canon Blast and Pastor Kitchen. Finally he told them of how well they had been received and that many Oldies and Littlekids through their own choice had become Voice followers.

Buddy now forgot about his anger against Miraclekid; he and Rhoda were impressed and very excited at what the Voice was doing in this town. 'What have they done to the Ancient Church of the Thirteenth Male Apostle and the Modern Movement of the Free Sisters' Fellowship buildings?' asked Buddy inquisitively.

'Well, one of the conditions that we were allowed to stay was that we must not use any buildings that would remind them of the bad old days, which of course suited us,' continued Hearthunter. 'But I believe the Sisters' building has now become a community cinema and the Males' building, which of course has the advantage of a high ceiling, is now being used as a badminton hall.'

'But what are they going to call the town if they don't want to be known as Religios-city?'

'That's an interesting one,' butted in Ivor. 'They are still discussing that, but they haven't told us anything.'

At this point Hope and Joy walked in, having finished their lesson, and again it was hugs all round. As they all gave thanks to the Voice, Buddy was aware that the Voice was speaking to them. 'We must find Angela and Miraclekid,' Buddy said. 'Being the cautious type of person I am,' he continued, 'I wouldn't usually do this, but Ivor, I want you to continue to oversee the work here as you have a little more experience than Hope and Joy, but I want them to stay here and support you.' All three looked pleased at being given such major responsibilities at such young ages. 'Well, the Voice seems to be using younger and younger Littlekids nowadays, so I'm certainly not going to put a cork on what he's doing. Hearthunter, Rhoda and I will go and try to find the other two, as I feel they are both in great danger.'

After more prayer and a few practical instructions Buddy, Hearthunter and Rhoda left the three Littlekids and set off. 'Where are we heading for?' asked Rhoda.

'Well, Runaway Forest seems as good a place to start as any,' said Buddy. But he really had no idea how they were going to find their two friends.

14

Foes 'n' Friends

After Little Chris had unwrapped Angela, he carefully lifted her up and helped her onto the sofa. He made a couple of hot drinks and a plate of cheese sandwiches (he remembered they were Angela's favourites). Then they started to say sorry to each other. Tears were flowing freely down both their faces as Angela began apologising for the terrible things she had thought about Little Christian back in Newchurch all that time ago. Little Chris butted in to say sorry for running away. Miraclekid had told him that Angela was really sorry, but he wanted her to suffer as he had done.

Angela picked up the story at that point and explained how from that time onwards she had lived under a cloud of guilt and had not been able to be part of Newchurch or be in contact with the Voice.

'It was all my fault,' wailed Little Chris. 'I'm sorry. The suffering I must have put you through.' Little Chris knelt down and held Angela's hand gently. 'Do you know I've been part of Nochurch since I left you? I even made everyone call me Little Chris because I knew deep down I wasn't right with the Voice, but from now on I want to be called Little Christian again.'

'Can you forgive me?' they both said to each other at the same time.

'Of course,' they both replied, still at the same time.

'I think now it's time we said sorry to the Voice,' said Little Christian. 'Hopefully it's not too late to put right all the things we have done wrong.'

Angela and Little Christian spent a long time confessing to the Voice, and the Voice assured both of them that not only were they forgiven, but he had a very important task for them to do, which he would tell them about as they read the Manual together over the next few days.

For hours they shared stories. Angela shared how she had been captured by a horrible muscular female Littlekid called Yolander in Runaway Forest, who had stolen her prize photograph from her. She then told of how she had been a slave of the horrible Major Snob-Value. She wept as she told it, still feeling the deep pain he had inflicted on her.

Little Christian explained how he had become rich by ripping off weak Nochurch Voice followers who watched his television show.

'I always thought ya were a star,' smiled Angela, wiping away her tears.

Little Christian smiled.

'Oh dear, what 'ave ya done to yer tongue?' she asked. 'There's an 'ole in it.'

Little Christian went bright red with guilt and embarrassment. He walked over and picked up the other package that had arrived with Angela. Tearing it open he allowed the Goosey uniform to fall onto the carpet.

'Yer a Goosey!' said Angela in disbelief.

'Yes, I'm afraid so,' confessed Little Christian. 'You see, in Nochurch all the top people are. It was the only way for me to be among the elite, which was where my stupid pride wanted me to be.'

'Ya must resign straightaway,' said Angela. 'They're evil. They're the lot what captured me, and I dare say many uvver Littlekids, and made us their slaves.'

'It's not that easy, Angela,' whispered Little Christian. 'If I do resign they will kill me—and probably you as well.'

As they both sat quietly thinking, Angela noticed the half-empty pill bottle. 'What are these for?' she asked.

Again Little Christian blushed. 'What I haven't told you is that I am no longer a star. I am now a nothing. Since I joined the Gooseys everything has gone wrong. I've been sacked from my TV programme, I've been ill, I have no money and will very shortly be thrown out of this wonderful house. A friend called Ron Guidance gave me those pills so that I could get away from all these problems by ending it all. If you'd arrived five minutes later I would have been dead.'

Again both went silent, but this time Angela

leaned over and squeezed his hand reassuringly. Angela and Little Christian had no answers to the dangerous situation they were in, but as time passed and as they continued to talk to the Voice together and read his Manual, he started giving them some. But they were answers that were going to require a lot of bravery and trust.

'Well, here we are in the middle of Runaway Forest, but what do we do now? Please, Voice, tell us,' prayed Buddy desperately.

'I think we should spread out and try to find some horse and cart tracks,' suggested Hearthunter, 'and then follow them. After all, that was the last thing we saw Miraclekid doing.' All agreed that this was a good idea and they spread out to search for tracks.

It wasn't long before Rhoda was heard shouting out excitedly, 'Look over here! It hasn't been long since the horse passed this way.'

'How can you be sure of that?' asked Buddy, as he and Hearthunter ran over to where she was.

'Well,' she said pointing, 'that mound of brown stuff over there is still steaming, so the horse must have dropped it fairly recently.'

As they all stared at the fresh horse dung Buddy said, 'Thank you, Rhoda,' and quickly changed the subject. 'Let's get moving then.'

They walked along, their eyes glued to the grass in front of them, frightened that they may take the wrong track, when again Rhoda made them both jump by shouting, 'Look—over there!'

They both looked up and saw a horse happily grazing at the edge of the path, while a rather muscular female Littlekid was sitting on the cart looking very miserable with her head in her hands.

'We will ask her if she has seen Angela or Miraclekid,' said Buddy, walking briskly up to the cart and taking control of the situation.

'Excuse me,' he said politely as he stood facing the Littlekid.

'What?' came the rude reply.

'I say,' Buddy continued, 'have you seen a couple of friends of ours?'

'I haven' t seen anyone for ages,' she said glumly.

'Well, it would have been quite some time ago actually,' said Hearthunter taking over. Then he started to describe Miraclekid. 'A male Littlekid, would have been about my height, totally fearless and always asking the Voice to do things to other people.'

Suddenly she looked up. 'Yes,' she said. 'What did you say his name was?'

'Oh, I don't think we did,' continued Buddy, happy that they were getting a response. 'His name is Miraclekid.'

'That must have been him,' said the Littlekid jumping down off the cart. 'I captured him, beat him up a bit, then gave him over to Bigsby Bankbalance of the Gooseys to take back to Nochurch.'

'You did what?' shouted Rhoda. 'You beat up our friend? How could you?' Then staring at her muscles she could see how easily she could.

Both Hearthunter and Buddy knew about the Gooseys and the evil deeds they were involved in. Buddy stared at the Littlekid, looking very stern. 'You realise that it's very likely that Miraclekid has been sold to become a Littlekid slave and sent far away. The Gooseys have contacts all round the world.'

The female Littlekid burst into tears. 'I really am

sorry,' she said. 'I've captured a lot of Littlekids for the Gooseys, but your friend seemed different from anyone else I've ever met. You see, I've never had any friends, and I think that he could have been my first one. I've not been able to capture anyone else since him. I feel so rotten.'

The Newchurch Littlekids looked at her, not knowing what to say. 'What's your name?' said Buddy eventually, feeling both guilty himself at the way he had spoken to her and compassionate for the situation she was in. He gently put his hand on her shoulder, which scared her as she had never been shown affection before.

'I'm Yolander Onmyturf,' she replied.

'Well, Yolander,' said Hearthunter, getting everyone out of the pastoral care mode, 'I suggest that you and we climb up on your cart and you get your horse moving at full throttle, I mean full gallop, and take us straight to Bigsby's bank. Who knows, we might still get there in time to rescue Miraclekid before the Gooseys export him.'

Yolander agreed, and in no time they were racing at breakneck speed through the forest towards Nochurch.

15

Wheels within Wheels

'Everything OK, Ron?'

'Yes, fine thanks, Bigsby. Have you got my package? My car is waiting outside the bank.'

Bigsby walked towards the open door of the vault and saw a wriggling large brown parcel on the floor.

'He's a lively one,' commented Ron.

'Yes, he certainly is,' agreed Bigsby, 'and a powerful one. I will be relieved to get him out of my bank. He should fetch a good price from our overseas agents.'

Bigsby grabbed one end of the parcel while Ron

grabbed the other, and with great difficulty they dragged it out into the street and put it onto the back seat of Ron's car, slamming the door behind it. 'Well, I must dash—I've got a meeting to attend,' said Bigsby, carrying a plastic bag with his Goosey gear under his arm.

'I understand,' said Ron, winking. 'I'll just take my parcel to the docks and wish it bon voyage.' They shook hands then went their separate ways.

It was rush hour again in Nochurch. In fact, with far too many cars for far too few roads, every hour was rush hour in Nochurch. Chief Kleencop took his cap off and scratched his head. 'This is all I need,' he shouted, looking at the cart with three wheels on it while the fourth had broken free from its axel and was racing down a hill chasing a large grey fluffy cat. The four Littlekids stood next to him, staring hopelessly at the place where the wheel once was. Nightmare the horse just stood still, waiting for Yolander to give it its next instructions.

'These contraptions should be banned in cities!' yelled the Chief. 'I've got enough trouble with motor vehicles.'

With that, the quickly-growing jam of motor vehicles started hooting their horns even more loudly. 'Why did you have to lose your wheel in the middle of the busiest crossroads in town? Ah well,' he mumbled, 'we ain't going to move you quickly, so I'd better move the rest of these cars then put a road block up and divert the traffic.'

They watched as Kleencop wandered down the queue of traffic and they could hear all the drivers moaning and swearing at him. Then he stopped alongside a large red car and was looking in the back window and shouting something to the driver. The driver got out while the Chief opened the back door and was leaning in the car.

'Oh oh, this looks like trouble,' observed Hearthunter, and all of them ran over to see what was happening.

'Look!' shouted Rhoda as the driver pulled a large heavy jack handle out of the front of the car and raised it above the cop's head. Suddenly, before he could bring it down and crack the skull of the officer, strong muscular arms had grabbed his arm and the heavy handle fell harmlessly into the road. Yolander twisted his arm high up his back as the cop leapt back out, realising that he had nearly been a gonner.

'Thanks, Littlekid,' Kleencop said, snapping his cuffs on the smartly-dressed Oldie with grey hair and a thin grey moustache, 'Now, before I throw you in the slammer, perhaps you would like to tell me who you are and why you have a Littlekid wrapped up in the back of your car?'

'It's me!' shouted a wriggling Miraclekid, who had managed to bite through the paper, roll off the back seat and get jammed on the floor between the front and back seats.

Buddy was both surprised and relieved, and along with Hearthunter and Rhoda gave thanks to the Voice there and then in the middle of the road for leading them to Miraclekid and for his safety. Yolander didn't know the Voice, but she did know Miraclekid, so she leapt enthusiastically onto the back seat and started unwrapping him.

The hooting was getting louder, but Chief Kleencop ignored it as Miraclekid managed to pull himself free from the wrapping paper and Yolander's clutches, and explained to him that he was on his way to the docks to be sold as a slave, and all under the instruction and for the benefit of the Gooseys.

'This could be just the break I need to bust the lot of them,' thought an excited Police Chief. Grabbing the driver, he asked him what his name was.

'Ron,' said the driver, now very frightened. 'Ron Guidance.'

'So you're a Goosey, are you?' shouted Chief Kleencop.

'Oh no,' said Ron, almost in tears. 'I'm just their delivery man.'

'Well, tell me where I can find the Gooseys,' he continued.

'I can't,' said Ron, now blubbing like a baby. 'They will kill me.'

'Well it's your choice. Either you take their blame and I throw the book at you, or you let them take their own blame and I will be much more lenient with you.'

'All right,' wailed Ron. 'It's a fair cop. You'll find them in the Oddboys' Hall. Just don't hurt me and don't let them hurt me. I can't stand pain.'

'Excellent,' said the Chief, as more officers arrived to take away the quivering Ron Guidance and to try and get the traffic moving again.

'OK, you Littlekids, jump into my squad car. We have a visit to make.'

'But what about my horse and cart?' asked Yolander.

'Yes, good point. It's probably better if you stay as the horse knows you. I'm sure my boys will help you take them both safely back to the station,' said the Chief, smiling.

16

The Big Ending

'All quiet!' shouted Grand Gander as he stood up and tried to squeeze in behind his table. All the gaggle stared at him and gasped. Realising what they were looking at he explained to them that he had a bit of a weight problem, which now accounted for him being the size of a barrage balloon. 'To continue,' he said, trying to change the subject, 'you may have noticed that we are back to our good old number of sixty-five.'

'Where's our new member?' shouted A Theist, forgetting to get permission to speak as usual.

'I'm afraid he wasn't really up to being one of us and he never really recovered after the initiation ceremony.'

'Permission to speak?' asked Al Kidsarbrats.

'What is it, Al?' said Grand Gander.

'Well, you were a bit rough on him at the initiation. I mean, none of us had to go through what he went through, did we?'

All the gaggle nodded in agreement.

'Oh dear,' said Grand Gander, 'I have gathered here the finest brains in all of Nochurch, but not one person has any idea of how my mind works. Listen, you fools, did you really think I wanted him here with us? As you know, I am not human like you. I am one of the Enemy Superpowers and Little Chris, or Little Christian as he was once known, in his heyday gave us more problems than anyone on the face of the earth. He humiliated my dear father, he blew up Oldchurch, he founded and led Newchurch, and every plan we made to destroy the Children of the you-know-who, he always discovered it and foiled us, making us look like a bunch of halfwits.

'But then his best friends did something to bring him down that we could never do. They really hurt him. Our job was then simple. All we had to do was to make sure that he would not forgive them. Our good friend Ron Guidance directed him away from the security of Newchurch to become a lone-ranger in Nochurch. Without a church he became weak and vulnerable.

'Hugo Yourway then came into the picture, and although we would all agree that he is a little strange, we would also agree that he does his job well. Little Chris became a TV star with all the trimmings. He had such a big ego, he didn't even miss his friends.

But I knew all along that his ego would not be satisfied until he joined us, the aristocracy of Nochurch. Then it was my turn. I broke him till he felt more useless than a worm. I took away his fame, his fans, his fortune and finally his future.'

Grand Gander took out the contract signed by Little Chris and as he tore it into little pieces he whispered, 'Little Chris will bother us no more. Little Chris has committed suicide.'

At that very moment the door burst open, knocking one of the Pecks flying, and a male and a female Littlekid ran into the middle of the room. 'Gooseys, I destroy you in the name of the Voice!' shouted Little Christian and immediately all the gaggle fell to the floor in fear, screaming and holding their ears.

'I destroy yer evil slave-trade and every uvver evil that yer've instigated, in the name of the Voice!' screamed Angela above the rising din.

The Pecks tried to approach and silence Little Christian and his Lesserbreed accomplice, but the Voice had paralysed them. Little Christian leapt onto the nearest table and ran down them till he came face to face with a very fat, very scared, very sweaty Grand Gander, who was so big he couldn't move anywhere.

'So we meet again, Grand Gander—or, judging by the size of you, and your generally ugly appearance, should I say a young Greedy Gutrot?'

'How did you manage to live?' stammered Gutrot.

'Easy. The Voice sent me a little present in my time of need,' he said, his face now radiant and glancing over at Angela. 'She gave me the will to live.

'Now it's time for you to leave Nochurch for ever. I think they have had enough of your evil influence, don't you? In the name of the Voice I call down fire from heaven. Burn him, Voice, and make him and all the evil he represents disappear.'

A thunderbolt shot straight through the ceiling of the Oddboys' Hall and all that was left of the devilish dictator was a pile of burned ash on his chair. All went instantly quiet.

'Bravo, Bravo!' came a lone voice from the back of the hall. 'I couldn't have done better myself.'

Little Christian spun around and saw his old friend Miraclekid looking up at him.

'Yea, not bad for a Littlekid!' shouted Buddy, Hearthunter and Rhoda all together.

While Chief Kleencop arrested all the gaggle and the Pecks and put them into waiting vans outside the building, he told them to take their last look at daylight, because where they were going they were not likely to see it again for a very long time.

Little Christian hugged each one of his friends in turn and, weeping with joy, apologised to them, explaining how everyone needed real friends, and how they were the best friends anyone could wish to have.

'You'd better believe it,' they all replied with wet eyes as well.

Then while the Police Chief personally cuffed and escorted his one-time friend Pat Rolman to the last van, all the Children of the Voice gave thanks both for his protection and for bringing them all back together again. As the Chief returned to the hall to make sure that he had not left any behind, he mentioned that he only had sixty-four. Would the fat one be returning? Everyone smiled and shouted that they hoped not. He then asked if they'd like a reward.

As Buddy started to explain that their reward was serving the Voice, Hearthunter and Miraclekid, never wanting to miss an opportunity, took the policeman to one side, out of everyone's earshot, and asked if as a reward they could return later in the year to tell the Nochurch people how they were missing out by not having a Newchurch in their city. The Chief shook their hands and said, 'It's a deal. I'll even help you arrange it.'

When they rejoined the others Buddy was suspicious and asked Miraclekid, 'What was all that about?'

'Oh, I'll tell you later,' he said, smiling and winking at Hearthunter.

The Chief gave them a lift to the Police Station where a smiling Yolander was waiting for them with Nightmare and a repaired cart. 'Anyone want a lift home?' she shouted. As Angela was about to ask what she was doing there they all shouted, 'Yes please!' and jumped up on the cart.

'Don't worry, I'll explain,' said Rhoda as the cart moved off, with a very grateful Chief Kleencop and many other honest policemen waving to them.

17

The Burning Question

'Never mind, Junior,' said the old fat Gutrot to the young fat Gutrot.

'But, Dad, I so nearly had him,' wailed Junior.

'Yes, I know the feeling,' said Senior.

'Perhaps if you hadn't been such a bigheaded arrogant young twit and listened to the wisdom of your old dad you may have succeeded.'

'Wisdom!' screamed Junior. 'I've got more wisdom lodged under my big toenail than you have in your enormous body.'

'Now, Junior, there's no need to get personal. By

the time you get to my age you will be twice my size. Anyway, let's not argue, because in the end we Enemy Superpowers will get him, Remember, there is always another day. . . .'

Greedy Gutrot Senior's face suddenly lit up. 'I've got it!' he shouted. 'Divided we failed, but what about if we teamed up, combined evil forces?'

Junior reached out, grabbed his father's hand and shook it in agreement, then smiled, 'It's a deal!'

Then Junior spoke very slowly. 'Father,' he growled, now we are partners, I would like to share with you a long-term plan that won't only destroy Little Christian, it could even knock Newchurch right back into Oldchurch in just a few years.'

Gutrot Senior stared at him in disbelief. 'How do you propose to do that?' he asked cynically.

'Simple,' said Junior. 'We wait patiently until Little Christian gets married and has Littlekids of his own. Then we will turn him into a nice normal family man.'

'It's a great thought, son,' he smiled. 'Once someone in Little Christian's position marries and settles down with his own Littlekids, it really does knock the heart out of the Voice's plans. There is, however, one slight flaw to your plan.'

'What's that?' enquired Junior.

'There's no chance of Little Christian getting married, blockhead.'

The Littlekids' Marching Song was sung so loudly it would have deafened anyone within a ten-mile radius. But that's not surprising, because Newchurch had so much to celebrate and to thank the Voice for. To start with, the Newchurch planted in Non-religios-city (at last they had decided upon a name, even if it was a very long one) was growing every day. Ivor Future, Hope Itgoeswell and Joy Atalltimes had so impressed Buddy with their leadership ability that they now lived there and had been asked to take responsibility for it indefinitely.

Hearthunter and Miraclekid had been given the all-clear from the Voice and Buddy to take a hit squad to Nochurch later in the year and had kept in close contact with Chief Kleencop, who was very close to becoming a really clean cop and a Voice follower himself.

Then there was Yolander Onmyturf, who had become a committed Voice follower and now lived in Newchurch, not her tree house. Of course she had to change Nightmare's name. She wanted to call it Gee Gee, but Buddy thought that Peaceful may be more appropriate. Yolander still had a slight problem in that she really fancied Miraclekid, who as yet had not returned the feelings. In fact, although he was known as the fearless one, some thought that the only person he was frightened of was Yolander.

But what made Newchurch most thankful to the Voice was the return of their founder leader Little Christian, along with Angela. Both were much closer to the Voice than they ever had been. Yes, there was a lot of praising and singing to be done by the Children of the Voice.

It was a burning hot Sunday afternoon. Little Christian and Angela were having a lazy afternoon walk through Runaway Forest. There was no fear in the forest now with Ron Guidance securely locked away and Yolander and Peaceful now happily living in Newchurch.

Little Christian slipped his hand into Angela's and

she giggled and blushed. She was not used to Little Christian showing any physical affection. He seemed to think it was a bad example for a leader to do that sort of thing when so many Littlekids were looking up to him. He stopped in the middle of the path and stood looking at her. 'I did miss you so much,' he said, his cheeks now starting to go red. 'I am so thankful to the Voice that he has given us another chance.'

Although Angela agreed, she kept quiet. She was enjoying listening to her friend's voice again and it was nice for her to hear him share his feelings, because she was never quite sure how he felt about her.

Eventually she did speak. 'What d'ya think the future 'olds for yer?' asked Angela.

'I don't know. The Voice hasn't told me yet. What about you?'

'I dunno,' Angela replied. 'The Voice 'asn't told me yet either.'

'Maybe we're not asking the Voice the right question,' continued Little Christian thoughtfully.

'What d'ya mean?' said Angela.

'Maybe we should be asking the Voice what the future holds for us.' And with that he kissed her on the lips. It was the first real kiss he'd ever given her— or anyone, for that matter—and although Angela was surprised that he would do such a thing, she felt warm and excited.

They stared at each other, then suddenly Angela shouted, 'Little Christian! Open yer mouth!'

Little Christian obediently opened wide, but was somewhat surprised by the request.

'Yep!' she beamed. 'It's gone! The 'ole in yer tongue 'as 'ealed over.'

Little Christian was so thrilled and relieved that a great big smile spread all over his face. 'Thank you, Voice. That was just the sort of sign I needed.'

'What d'ya mean, sign?' asked Angela looking at him suspiciously.

Little Christian kissed her again. 'It was as I kissed you that the Voice healed me. I believe that the Voice wants us to be together . . . permanently.'

'Angela, I love you . . . will you marry me?'

Before Angela could open her mouth to answer they were disturbed by two noisy Littlekids running towards them shouting.

'Slow down, Miraclekid,' yelled a puffed out Yolander trailing a few metres behind him. 'I only wanted to go for a short romantic walk—not a cross-country run.'

'Personally,' replied Miraclekid, keeping up the pace, 'I believe a good fast jog is much healthier for both of us, so stop moaning and save your breath for running.'

'Hi, Little Christian, Hi, Angela,' they both shouted as they ran past them. 'Hope we haven't interrupted anything.' Miraclekid and Yolander giggled as they disappeared into the distance.

Little Christian was now feeling a bit embarrassed. Proposing once was one thing, but proposing *twice*?

He glanced at Angela. She looked stunning, and that was all the encouragement he needed. Plucking up his courage for the second time he whispered, 'Angela, will you . . .?'

Before he could finish his sentence he jumped with surprise as he heard a familiar voice behind him. 'Angela! Little Christian! There you both are. We've been trying to find you for ages.'

Hearthunter and Buddy were walking briskly

towards them. 'I hope we're not disturbing you,' continued Buddy. 'But we have a female Littlekid who needs a bit of encouragement. Normally I'd ask Harmony but she seems to have gone for a ride on Peaceful. If you're not involved in anything too important, Angela, I wondered if you could come and have a word with her.

Angela glanced at Little Christian, her eyes sparkling in the sunlight, and then she smiled a warm smile. 'Of course I will, Buddy,' she answered. 'Nothing is more important than working for the Voice, is it?' and with that she squeezed Little Christian's hand and walked off with Buddy.

Hearthunter stood next to his friend and slapped him playfully on the shoulder, 'We didn't come at an inappropriate moment, did we?' he asked. 'I mean, you weren't discussing something important, were you?'

Little Christian stood quietly for a moment watching Angela disappearing in the distance. He shrugged his shoulders. 'Nothing is more important than working for the Voice, is it?'

'Spoken like a true leader,' grinned Hearthunter. 'Come on, wake up, loverboy.' With that he gave the thoughtful Little Christian a hefty thump. Little Christian lost his balance and toppled into a muddy ditch by the side of the path.

Laughing at his rude awakening from cloud nine, Little Christian tried to pick himself up, but could only slide about in the slippery mud. 'You wait till I get my hands on you!' he shouted.

'Again, spoken like a true leader,' repeated Hearthunter, chuckling and retreating down the path. 'But you will have to catch me first.'

The two friends chased each other back to Newchurch, laughing all the way.